In The Amazon Jungle

Algot Lange

Contents

IN THE AMAZON JUNGLE

BY

Algot Lange

To
The Memory of
My Father

INTRODUCTION

When Mr. Algot Lange told me he was going to the headwaters of the Amazon, I was particularly interested because once, years ago, I had turned my own mind in that direction with considerable longing. I knew he would encounter many set-backs, but I never would have predicted the adventures he actually passed through alive.

He started in fine spirits: buoyant, strong, vigorous. When I saw him again in New York, a year or so later, on his return, he was an emaciated fever-wreck, placing one foot before the other only with much exertion and indeed barely able to hold himself erect. A few weeks in the hospital, followed by a daily diet of quinine, improved his condition, but after months he had scarcely arrived at his previous excellent physical state.

Many explorers have had experiences similar to those related in this volume, but, at least so far as the fever and the cannibals are concerned, they have seldom survived to tell of them. Their interviews with cannibals have been generally too painfully confined to internal affairs to be available in this world for authorship, whereas Mr. Lange, happily, avoided not only a calamitous intimacy, but was even permitted to view the culinary preparations relating to the absorption of less favoured individuals, and himself could have joined the feast, had he possessed the stomach for it. These good friends of his, the Mangeromas, conserved his life when they found him almost dying, not, strange as it may appear, for selfish banqueting purposes, but merely that he might return to his own people. It seems rather paradoxical that they should have loved one stranger so well as to spare him with suspicious kindness, and love others to the extent of making them into table delicacies. The explanation probably is that these Mangeromas were the reverse of a certain foreign youth with only a small stock of English, who, on being offered in New York a fruit he had never seen before, replied, "Thank you, I eat only my acquaintances"--the Mangeromas eat only their enemies.

Mr. Lange's account of his stay with these people, of their weapons, habits, form of battle, and method of cooking the human captives, etc., forms one of the specially interesting parts of the book, and is at the same time a valuable contribution to the ethnology of the western Amazon (or Maranon) region, where dwell numerous similar tribes little known to the white man. Particularly notable is his description of the wonderful wourahli (urari) poison, its extraordinary effect, and the ***modus operandi*** of its making; a poison used extensively by Amazonian tribes but not made by all. He describes also the bows and arrows, the war-clubs, and the very scientific weapon, the blow-gun. He was fortunate in securing a photograph of a Mangeroma in the act of shooting this gun. Special skill, of course, is necessary for the effective use of this simple but terrible arm, and, like that required for the boomerang or lasso, practice begins with childhood.

The region of Mr. Lange's almost fatal experiences, the region of the Javary River (the boundary between Brazil and Peru), is one of the most formidable and least known portions of the South American continent. It abounds with obstacles to exploration of the most overwhelming kind. Low, swampy, with a heavy rainfall, it is inundated annually, like most of the Amazon basin, and at time of high water the rivers know no limits. Lying, as it does, so near the equator, the heat is intense and constant, oppressive even to the native. The forest-growth--and it is forest wherever it is not river--is forced as in a huge hothouse, and is so dense as to render progress through it extremely difficult. Not only are there obstructions in the way of tree trunks, underbrush, and trailing vines and creepers like ropes, but the footing is nothing more than a mat of interlaced roots. The forest is also sombre and gloomy. To take a photograph required an exposure of from three to five minutes. Not a stone, not even a pebble, is anywhere to be found.

Disease is rampant, especially on the smaller branches of the rivers. The incurable ***beri-beri*** and a large assortment of fevers claim first place as death dealers, smiting the traveller with fearful facility. Next come a myriad of insects and reptiles--alligators, huge bird-eating spiders, and snakes of many varieties. Snakes, both the poisonous and non-poisonous kinds, find here conditions precisely to their liking. The bush-master is met with in the more open places, and there are many that are venomous, but the most terrifying, though not a biting reptile is the water-boa, the sucuruju (***Eunectes murinus***) or anaconda. It lives to a great age and reaches a size almost beyond belief. Feeding, as generally it does at night, it escapes common observation, and white men, heretofore, have not seen the largest specimens reported, though more than thirty feet is an accepted length, and Bates, the English naturalist, mentions one he heard of, forty-two feet long. It is not surprising that Mr. Lange should have met with one in the far wilderness he visited, of even greater proportions, a hideous monster, ranking in its huge bulk with the giant beasts of antediluvian times. The sucuruju is said to be able to swallow whole animals as large as a goat or a donkey, or even larger, and the naturalist referred to tells of a ten-year-old boy, son of his neighbour, who, left to mind a canoe while his father went into the forest, was, in broad day, playing in the shade of the trees, stealthily enwrapped by one of the monsters. His cries brought his father to the rescue just in time.

As the Javary heads near the eastern slopes and spurs of the great Peruvian Cordillera, where once lived the powerful and wealthy Inca race with their great stores of pure gold obtained from prolific mines known to them, it is again not surprising that Mr. Lange should have stumbled upon a marvellously rich deposit of the precious metal in a singular form. The geology of the region is unknown and the origin of the gold Mr. Lange found cannot at present even be surmised.

Because of the immense value of the rubber product, gold attracts less attention than it would in some other country. The rubber industry is extensive and thousands of the wild rubber trees are located and tapped. The trees usually are found near streams and the search for them leads the rubber-hunter farther and farther into the unbroken wilderness. Expeditions from time to time are sent out by rich owners of rubber "estates" to explore for fresh trees, and after his sojourn at Remate de Males and Floresta, so full of interest, Mr. Lange accompanied one of these parties into the unknown, with the extraordinary results described so simply yet dramatically in the following pages, which I commend most cordially, both to the experienced explorer and to the stay-by-the-fire, as an unusual and exciting story of adventure.

FREDERICK S. DELLENBAUGH.
NEW YORK, November 24, 1911.

PREFACE

It is difficult, if not impossible, to find a more hospitable and generous nation than the Brazilian. The recollection of my trip through the wilds of Amazonas lingers in all its details, and although my experiences were not always of a pleasant character, yet the good treatment and warm reception accorded me make me feel the deepest sense of gratitude to the Brazilians, whose generosity will always abide in my memory.

There is in the Brazilian language a word that better than any other describes the feeling with which one remembers a sojourn in Brazil. This word, *saudades*, is charged with an abundance of sentiment, and, though a literal translation of it is difficult to arrive at, its meaning approaches "sweet memories of bygone days."

Although a limitation of space forbids my expressing in full my obligation to all those who treated me kindly, I must not omit to state my special indebtedness to three persons, without whose invaluable assistance and co-operation I would not have been able to complete this book.

First of all, my thanks are due to the worthy Colonel Rosendo da Silva, owner of the rubber estate Floresta on the Itecoahy River. Through his generosity and his interest, I was enabled to study the work and the life conditions of the rubber workers, the employees on his estate.

The equally generous but slightly less civilised Benjamin, high potentate of the tribe of Mangeroma cannibals, is the second to whom I wish to express my extreme gratitude, although my obligations to him are of a slightly different character: in the first place, because he did not order me to be killed and served up, well or medium done, to suit his fancy (which he had a perfect right to do); and, in the second place, because he took a great deal of interest in my personal welfare and bestowed all the strange favours upon me that are recorded in this book. He opened my eyes to things which, at the time and under the circumstances, did not impress me much, but which, nevertheless, convinced me that, even at this late period of the world's history, our earth has not been reduced to a dead level of drab and commonplace existence, and that somewhere in the remote parts of the world are still to be found people who have never seen or heard of white men.

Last, but not least, I wish to express my deep obligation to my valued friend, Frederick S. Dellenbaugh, who, through his helpful suggestions, made prior to my departure, contributed essentially to the final success of this enterprise, and whose friendly assistance has been called into requisition and unstintingly given in the course of the preparation of this volume.

A.L.
NEW YORK, January, 1912.

CHAPTER I
REMATE DE MALES, OR "CULMINATION OF EVILS"

My eyes rested long upon the graceful white-painted hull of the R.M.S. *Manco* as she disappeared behind a bend of the Amazon River, more than 2200 miles from the Atlantic Ocean. After 47 days of continuous travel aboard of her, I was at last standing on the Brazilian frontier, watching the steamer's plume of smoke still hanging lazily over the immense, brooding forests. More than a plume of smoke it was to me then; it was the final link that bound me to the outside world of civilisation. At last it disappeared. I turned and waded through the mud up to a small wooden hut built on poles.

It was the end of January, 1910, that saw me approaching this house, built on Brazilian terra firma--or rather terra aqua, for water was inundating the entire land. I had behind me the Amazon itself, and to the right the Javary River, while the little house that I was heading for was Esperanca, the official frontier station of Brazil. The opposite shore was Peru and presented an unbroken range of dense, swampy forest, grand but desolate to look upon.

A middle-aged man in uniform came towards me and greeted me cordially, in fact embraced me, and, ordering a servant to pull my baggage out of the water, led me up a ladder into the house. I told him that I intended to go up the Javary River, to a place called Remate de Males, where I would live with a medical friend of mine, whereupon he informed me that a launch was due this same night, which would immediately proceed to my proposed destination. Later in the evening the launch came and I embarked after being once more embraced by the courteous Cor. Monteiro, the frontier official. The captain of this small trading launch was an equally hospitable and courteous man; he invited me into his cabin and tried to explain that this river, and the town in particular, where we were going, was a most unhealthy and forbidding place, especially for a foreigner, but he added cheerfully that he knew of one white man, an Englishman, who had succeeded in living for several years on the Javary without being killed by the fever, but incidentally had drank himself to death.

The night was very dark and damp, and I did not see much of the passing scenery; a towering black wall of trees was my total impression during the journey. However, I managed at length to fall asleep on some coffee-bags near the engine and did not wake till the launch was exhausting its steam supply through its whistle.

My next impression was that of a low river bank fringed with dirty houses lighted by candles. People were sitting in hammocks smoking cigarettes, dogs were barking incessantly, and frogs and crickets were making a deafening noise when I walked up the main and only street of this little town, which was to be my head-quarters for many months to come.

After some inquiry, I finally found my friend, Dr. M----, sitting in a dark, dismal room in the so-called *Hotel Agosto*. With a graceful motion of his hand he pointed to a chair of ancient structure, indicating that having now travelled so many thousand miles to reach this glorious place, I was entitled to sit down and let repose overtake me. Indeed, I was in Remate de Males.

Never shall I forget that first night's experience with mosquitoes and ants. Besides this my debut in a hammock for a bed was a pronounced failure, until a merciful sleep temporarily took me from the sad realities.

Remate de Males lies just where a step farther would plunge one into an unmapped country. It is a little village built on poles; the last "blaze" of civilisation on the trail of the upper river. When the rainy winter season drives out of the forests every living creature that can not take refuge in the trees, the rubber-workers abandon the crude stages of the manufacture that they carry on there and gather in the village to make the best of what life has to offer them in this region. At such times the population rises to the number of some 500 souls, for the most part Brazilians and domesticated Indians or *caboclos*.

Nothing could better summarise the attractions (!) of the place than the name which has become fixed upon it. Translated into English this means "Culmination of Evils," Remate de Males.

Some thirty years ago, a prospector with his family and servants, in all about a score, arrived at this spot near the junction of the Javary and the Itecoahy rivers, close to the equator. They came by the only possible highway, the river, and decided to settle. Soon the infinite variety of destroyers of human life that abound on the upper Amazon began their work on the little household, reducing its number to four and threatening to wipe it out altogether. But the prospector stuck to it and eventually succeeded in giving mankind a firm hold on this wilderness. In memory of what he and succeeding settlers went through, the village received its cynically descriptive name.

Remate de Males, separated by weeks and weeks of journey by boat from the nearest spot of comparative civilisation down the river, has grown wonderfully since its pioneer days. Dismal as one finds it to be, if I can give an adequate description in these pages, it will be pronounced a monument to man's nature-conquering instincts, and ability. Surely no pioneers ever had a harder battle than these Brazilians, standing with one foot in "the white man's grave," as the Javary region is called in South America, while they faced innumerable dangers. The markets of the world need rubber, and the supplying of this gives them each year a few months' work in the forests at very high wages. I always try to remember these facts when I am tempted to harshly judge Remate de Males according to our standards; moreover, I can never look upon the place quite as an outsider. I formed pleasant friendships there and entered into the lives of many of its people, so I shall always think of it with affection. The village is placed where the Itecoahy runs at right angles into the Javary, the right-hand bank of the Itecoahy forming at once its main and its only street. The houses stand facing this street, all very primitive and all elevated on palm-trunk poles as far as possible above the usual high-water mark of the river. Everything, from the little sheet-iron church to the pig-sty, is built on poles. Indeed, if there is anything in the theory of evolution, it will not be many generations before the inhabitants and domestic animals are born equipped with stilts.

Opposite Remate de Males, across the Itecoahy, is a collection of some ten huts that form the village of Sao Francisco, while across the Javary is the somewhat larger village of Nazareth. Like every real metropolis, you see, Remate de Males has its suburbs. Nazareth is in Peruvian territory, the Javary forming the boundary between Brazil and Peru throughout its length of some 700 miles. This same boundary line is a source of amusing punctiliousness between the officials of each country. To cross it is an affair requiring the exercise of the limits of statesmanship. I well remember an incident that occurred during my stay in the village. A sojourner in our town, an Indian rubber-worker from the Ituhy River, had murdered a woman by strangling her. He escaped in a canoe to Nazareth before the Brazilian officials could capture him, and calmly took refuge on the porch of a house there, where he sat down in a hammock and commenced to smoke cigarettes, feeling confident that his pursuers would not invade Peruvian soil. But local diplomacy was equal to the emergency. Our officials went to the shore opposite Nazareth, and, hiding behind the trees, endeavoured to pick off their man with their .44 Winchesters, reasoning that though their crossing would be an international incident, no one could object to a bullet's crossing. Their poor aim was the weak spot in the plan. After a few vain shots had rattled against the sheet-iron walls of the house where the fugitive was sitting, he got up from among his friends and lost himself in the jungle, never to be heard of again.

About sixty-five houses, lining the bank of the Itecoahy River over a distance of what would be perhaps six blocks in New York City, make up Remate de Males. They are close together and each has a ladder reaching from the street to the main and only floor. At the bottom of every ladder appears a rudimentary pavement, probably five square feet in area and consisting of fifty or sixty whiskey and gin bottles placed with their necks downwards. Thus in the rainy season when the water covers the street to a height of seven feet, the ladders always have a solid foundation. The floors consist of split palm logs laid with the round side up. Palm leaves form the roofs, and rusty corrugated sheet-iron, for the most part, the walls. Each house has a sort of backyard and kitchen, also on stilts and reached by a bridge.

Through the roofs and rafters gambol all sorts of wretched pests. Underneath the houses roam pigs, goats, and other domestic animals, which sometimes appear in closer proximity than might be wished, owing to the spaces between the logs of the floor. That is in the dry season. In the winter, or the wet season, these animals are moved into the houses with you, and their places underneath are occupied by river creatures, alligators, water-snakes, and malignant, repulsive fish, of which persons outside South America know nothing.

Near the centre of the village is the "sky-scraper," the *Hotel de Augusto*, which boasts a story and a quarter in height. Farther along are the *Intendencia*, or Government building, painted blue, the post-office yellow, the *Recreio Popular* pink; beyond, the residence of Mons. Danon, the plutocrat of the village, and farther "downtown" the church, unpainted. Do not try to picture any of these places from familiar structures. They are all most unpretentious; their main point of difference architecturally from the rest of the village consists in more utterly neglected facades.

The post-office and the meteorological observatory, in one dilapidated house, presided over by a single self-important official, deserve description here. The postmaster himself is a pajama-clad gentleman, whose appearance is calculated to strike terror to the souls of humble *seringueiros*, or rubber-workers, who apply for letters only at long intervals. On each of these occasions I would see this important gentleman, who had the word *coronel* prefixed to his name, Joao Silva de Costa Cabral, throw up his hands, in utter despair at being disturbed, and slowly proceed to his desk from which he would produce the letters. With great pride this "Pooh-Bah" had a large sign painted over the door. The post-office over which he presides is by no means overworked, as only one steamer arrives every five weeks, or so, but still he has the appearance of being "driven." But when he fusses around his "*Observatorio meteorologico*," which consists of a maximum and minimum thermometer and a pluviometer, in a tightly closed box, raised above the ground on a tall pole, then indeed, his air would impress even the most blase town-sport. I was in the village when this observatory was installed, and after it had been running about a week, the mighty official called on me and asked me confidentially if I would not look the observatory over and see if it was all right.

My examination showed that the thermometers were screwed on tight, which accounted for the amazingly uniform readings shown on his chart. The pluviometer was inside the box, and therefore it would have been difficult to convince scientists that the clouds had not entirely skipped Remate de Males during the rainy season, unless the postmaster were to put the whole observatory under water by main force. He also had a chart showing the distribution of clouds on each day of the year. I noticed that the letter "N" occupied a suspiciously large percentage of the space on the chart, and when I asked him for the meaning of this he said that "N"--

which in meteorological abbreviation means Nimbus--stood for "**None**" (in Portuguese **Nao**). And he thought that he must be right because it was the rainy season.

The hotel, in which I passed several months as a guest, until I finally decided to rent a hut for myself, had points about it which outdid anything that I have ever seen or heard of in comic papers about "summer boarding." The most noticeable feature was the quarter-of-a-story higher than any other house in the village. While this meant a lead as to quantity I could never see that it represented anything in actual quality. I would not have ventured up the ladder which gave access to the extra story without my Winchester in hand, and during the time I was there I never saw anyone else do so. The place was nominally a store-house, but having gone undisturbed for long periods it was an ideal sanctuary for hordes of vermin--and these the vermin of the Amazon, dangerous, poisonous, not merely the annoying species we know. Rats were there in abundance, also deadly scolopendra and centipedes; and large bird-eating spiders were daily seen promenading up and down the sheet-iron walls.

On the main floor the building had two large rooms across the centre, one on the front and one on the rear. At each side were four small rooms. The large front-room was used as a dining-room and had two broad tables of planed palm trunks. The side-rooms were bedrooms, generally speaking, though most of the time I was there some were used for stabling the pigs and goats, which had to be taken in owing to the rainy season.

It is a simple matter to keep a hotel on the upper Amazon. Each room in the **Hotel de Augusto** was neatly and chastely furnished with a pair of iron hooks from which to hang the hammock, an article one had to provide himself. There was nothing in the room besides the hooks. No complete privacy was possible because the corrugated sheet-iron partitions forming the walls did not extend to the roof. The floors were sections of palm trees, with the flat side down, making a succession of ridges with open spaces of about an inch between, through which the ground or the water, according to the season, was visible. The meals were of the usual monotonous fare typical of the region. Food is imported at an enormous cost to this remote place, since there is absolutely no local agriculture. Even sugar and rice, for instance, which are among the important products of Brazil, can be had in New York for about one-tenth of what the natives pay for them in Remate de Males. A can of condensed milk, made to sell in America for eight or nine cents, brings sixty cents on the upper Amazon, and preserved butter costs $1.20 a pound.

The following prices which I have had to pay during the wet season in this town will, doubtless, be of interest:

One box of sardines	$ 1.20
One pound of unrefined sugar	.30
One roll of tobacco (16 pounds)	21.30
One basket of farinha retails in Para for $4.50	13.30
One bottle of ginger ale	.60
One pound of potatoes	.60
Calico with stamped pattern, pr. yd.	.90
One Collins machete, N.Y. price, $1.00	12.00
One pair of men's shoes	11.00
One bottle of very plain port wine, 22,000 reis or	7.30

Under such circumstances, of course, the food supply is very poor. Except for a few dried cereals and staples, nothing is used but canned goods; the instances where small domestic animals are slaughtered are so few as to be negligible. Furthermore, as a rule, these very animals are converted into jerked meat to be kept for months and months. Some fish are taken from the river, but the Amazon fish are none too palatable generally speaking, with a few exceptions; besides, the natives are not skilful enough to prepare them to suit a civilised palate.

A typical, well provided table on the Amazon would afford dry farinha in the first place. This is the granulated root of the Macacheira plant, the ***Jatropha mani-hot***, which to our palates would seem like desiccated sawdust, although it appears to be a necessity for the Brazilian. He pours it on his meat, into his soup, and even into his wine and jams. Next you would have a black bean, which for us lacks flavour even as much as the farinha. With this there would probably be rice, and on special occasions jerked beef, a product as tender and succulent as the sole of a riding boot. Great quantities of coffee are drunk, made very thick and prepared without milk or sugar. All these dishes are served at once, so that they promptly get cold and are even more tasteless before their turn comes to be devoured.

For five months I experienced this torturing menu at the hotel with never-ceasing regularity. The only change I ever noticed was on Sundays or days of feast when beans might occupy the other end of the table.

But what can the Brazilians do? The cost of living is about ten times as high as in New York. Agriculture is impossible in the regions where the land is flooded annually, and the difficulties of shipping are enormous. When I left the hotel and started housekeeping on my own account, I found that I could not do a great deal better. By specialising on one thing at a time I avoided monotony to some extent, but then it was probably only because I was a "new broom" at the business.

As illustrating the community life that we enjoyed at the hotel, I will relate a happening that I have set down in my notes as an instance of the great mortality of this region. One afternoon a woman's three-months-old child was suddenly taken ill. The child grew worse rapidly and the mother finally decided that it was going to die. Her husband was up the river on the rubber estates and she did not want to be left alone. So she came to the hotel with the child and besought them to let her in. The infant was placed in a hammock where it lay crying pitifully. At last the wailings of the poor little creature became less frequent and the child died.

Before the body was quite cold the mother and the landlady commenced clearing a table in the dining-room. I looked at this performance in astonishment because it was now evident that they were going to prepare a "***lit de parade***" there, close to the tables where our meals were served. The body was then brought in, dressed in a white robe adorned with pink, yellow, and sky-blue silk ribbons. Loose leaves and branches were scattered over the little emaciated body, care being taken not to conceal any of the fancy silk ribbons. Empty whiskey and gin bottles were placed around the bier, a candle stuck in the mouth of each bottle, and then the whole thing was lighted up.

It was now getting dark fast, and as the doors were wide open, a great crowd was soon attracted by the brilliant display. All the "400" of the little rubber town seemed to pour in a steady stream into the dining-room. It was a new experience, even in this hotel where I had eaten with water up to my knees, to take a meal with a funeral going on three feet away. We had to partake of our food with the body close by and the candle smoke blowing in our faces, adding more local colour to our jerked beef and beans than was desirable. More and more people came in to pay their respects to the child that hardly any one had known while it was alive. Through it all the mother sat on a trunk in a corner peacefully smoking her pipe, evidently proud of the celebration that was going on in honour of her deceased offspring.

The kitchen boy brought in a large tray with cups of steaming coffee; biscuits also were carried around to the spectators who sat against the wall on wooden boxes. The women seemed to get the most enjoyment out of the mourning; drinking black coffee, smoking their pipes, and paying little attention to the cause of their being there, only too happy to have an official occasion to show off their finest skirts. The men had assembled around the other table, which had been cleared in the meantime, and they soon sent the boy out for whiskey and beer, passing away the time playing cards.

I modestly inquired how long this feast was going to last, because my room adjoined the dining-room and was separated only by a thin sheet-iron partition open at the top. The landlady, with a happy smile, informed me that the mourning would continue till the early hours, when a launch would arrive to transport the deceased and the guests to the cemetery. This was about four miles down the Javary River and was a lonely, half-submerged spot.

There was nothing for me to do but submit and make the best of it. All night the mourners went on, the women drinking black coffee, while the men gambled and drank whiskey in great quantities, the empty bottles being employed immediately as additional candlesticks. Towards morning, due to their heroic efforts, a multitude of bottles totally obliterated the "*lit de parade*" from view. I managed to fall asleep completely exhausted when the guests finally went off at nine o'clock. The doctor diagnosed the case of the dead child as chronic indigestion, the result of the mother's feeding a three-months-old infant on jerked beef and black beans.

Life in the hotel during the rainy season is variegated. I have spoken of having eaten a meal with water up to my knees. That happened often during the weeks when the river was at its highest level. Once when we were having our noon-day meal during the extreme high-water period a man came paddling his canoe in at the open door, sailed past us, splashing a little water on the table as he did so, and navigated through to the back room where he delivered some supplies.

During this feat everybody displayed the cheerful and courteous disposition usual to the Brazilians. At this season you must wear wading boots to eat a meal or do anything else about the house. Sleeping is somewhat easier as the hammocks are suspended about three feet above the level of the water, but an involuntary plunge is a thing not entirely unknown to an amateur sleeping in a hammock; I know this from personal experience.

Every morning the butcher comes to the village between five and six o'clock and sharpens his knife while he awaits calls for his ministrations. He is an under-sized man with very broad shoulders and a face remarkable for its cunning, cruel expression. His olive-brown complexion, slanting eyes, high cheek-bones, and sharp-filed teeth are all signs of his coming from the great unknown interior. His business here is to slaughter the cattle of the town. He does this deftly by thrusting a long-bladed knife into the neck of the animal at the base of the brain, until it severs the medulla, whereupon the animal collapses without any visible sign of suffering. It is then skinned and the intestines thrown into the water where they are immediately devoured by a small but voracious fish called the *candiroo-escrivao*. This whole operation is carried on inside the house, in the back-room, as long as the land is flooded.

It must be remembered that during the rainy season an area equal in size to about a third of the United States is entirely submerged. There is a network of rivers that eventually find their way into the Amazon and the land between is completely inundated. In all this immense territory there are only a few spots of sufficient elevation to be left high and dry. Remate de Males, as I have explained, is at the junction of the Itecoahy and the Javary rivers, the latter 700 miles in length, and thirty miles or so below the village the Javary joins the Amazon proper, or Solimoes as it is called here. Thus we are in the heart of the submerged region. When I first arrived in February, 1910, I found the river still confined to its channel, with the water about ten feet below the level of the street. A few weeks later it was impossible to take a single step on dry land anywhere.

The water that drives the rubber-workers out of the forests also drives all animal life to safety. Some of the creatures seek refuge in the village. I remember that we once had a huge alligator take temporary lodgings in the backyard of the hotel after he had travelled no one knows how many miles through the inundated forest. At all hours we could hear him making excursions under the house to snatch refuse thrown from the kitchen, but we always knew he would have welcomed more eagerly a member of the household who might drop his way.

And now a few words about the people who lived under the conditions I have described, and who keep up the struggle even though, as they themselves have put it, "each ton of rubber costs a human life."

In the first place I must correct any erroneous impression as to neatness that may have been formed by my remarks about the animals being kept in the dwellings during the rainy season. The Brazilians are scrupulous about their personal cleanliness, and in fact, go through difficulties to secure a bath which might well discourage more civilised folk.

No one would dream, for an instant, of immersing himself in the rivers. In nine cases out of ten it would amount to suicide to do so, and the natives have bathhouses along the shores; more literally bathhouses than ours, for their baths are actually taken in them. They are just as careful about clothing being aired and clean. Indeed, the main item of the Brazilian woman's housekeeping is the washing. The cooking is rather happy-go-lucky; and there is no use cleaning and polishing iron walls; they get rusty anyhow.

The people are all occupied with the rubber industry and the town owes its existence to the economic necessity of having here a shipping and trading point for the product. The rubber is gathered farther up along the shores of the Javary and the Itecoahy and is transported by launch and canoe to Remate de Males. Here it is shipped directly or sold to travelling dealers who send it down to Manaos or Para via the boat of the Amazon Steam Navigation Co., which comes up during the rainy season. Thence it goes to the ports of the world.

The rubber-worker is a well paid labourer even though he belongs to the unskilled class. The tapping of the rubber trees and the smoking of the milk pays from eight to ten dollars a day in American gold. This, to him, of course, is riches and the men labour here in order that they may go back to their own province as wealthy men. Nothing else will yield this return; the land is not used for other products. It is hard to see how agriculture or cattle-raising could be carried on in this region, and, if they could, they would certainly not return more than one fourth or one fifth of what the rubber industry does. The owners of the great rubber estates, or **seringales**, are enormously wealthy men.

There are fewer women than men in Remate de Males, and none of the former is beautiful. They are for the most part Indians or Brazilians from the province of Ceara, with very dark skin, hair, and eyes, and teeth filed like shark's teeth. They go barefooted, as a rule. Here you will find all the incongruities typical of a race taking the first step in civilisation. The women show in their dress how the well-paid men lavish on them the extravagances that appeal to the lingering savage left in their simple natures.

Women, who have spent most of their isolated lives in utterly uncivilised surroundings, will suddenly be brought into a community where other women are found, and immediately the instinct of self-adornment is brought into full play. Each of them falls under the sway of "Dame Fashion"--for there are the **latest things**, even on the upper Amazon. Screaming colours are favoured; a red skirt with green stars was considered at one time the height of fashion, until an inventive woman discovered that yellow dots could also be worked in. In addition to these dresses, the women will squander money on elegant patent-leather French slippers (with which they generally neglect to wear stockings), and use silk handkerchiefs perfumed with the finest Parisian eau de Cologne, bought at a cost of from fourteen to fifteen dollars a bottle. Arrayed in all her glory on some gala occasion, the whole effect enhanced by the use of a short pipe from which she blows volumes of smoke, the woman of Remate de Males is a unique sight.

CHAPTER II
THE SOCIAL AND POLITICAL LIFE OF REMATE DE MALES

The social life of the town is in about the same stage of development as it must have been during the Stone Age. When darkness falls over the village, as it does at six o'clock all the year round, life practically stops, and a few hours afterwards everyone is in his hammock.

There is one resort where the town-sports come to spend their evenings, the so-called *Recreio Popular*. Its principal patrons are *seringueiros*, or rubber-workers, who have large rolls of money that they are anxious to spend with the least possible effort, and generally get their desire over the gaming boards. The place is furnished with a billiard table and a gramophone with three badly worn records. The billiard table is in constant use by a certain element up to midnight, and so are the three eternal records of the gramophone. It will take me years surrounded by the comforts of civilisation to get those three frightful tunes out of my head, and I do not see how they could fail to drive even the hardened *seringueiros* to an early grave.

Another resort close by, where the native *cachassa* is sold, is patronised principally by negroes and half-breeds. Here they play the guitar, in combination with a home-made instrument resembling a mandolin, as accompaniment to a monotonous native song, which is kept up for hours. With the exception of these two places, the village does not furnish any life or local colour after nightfall, the natives spending their time around the mis-treated gramophones, which are found in almost every hut.

The men of the village, unlike the women, are not picturesque in appearance.

The officials are well paid, so is everyone else, yet they never think of spending money to improve the looks of the village or even their own. Most of them are ragged. A few exhibit an inadequate elegance, dressed in white suits, derby hats, and very high collars. But in spite of the seeming poverty, there is not a **seringueiro** who could not at a moment's notice produce a handful of bills that would strike envy to the heart of many prosperous business men of civilisation. The amount will often run into millions of reis; a sum that may take away the breath of a stranger who does not know that one thousand of these Brazilian reis make but thirty cents in our money.

The people of the Amazon love to gamble. One night three merchants and a village official came to the hotel to play cards. They gathered around the dining-room table at eight o'clock, ordered a case of Pabst beer, which sells, by the way, at four dollars and sixty cents a bottle in American gold, and several boxes of our National Biscuit Company's products, and then began on a game, which resembles our poker. They played till midnight, when they took a recess of half an hour, during which large quantities of the warm beer and many crackers were consumed. Then, properly nourished, they resumed the game, which lasted until six o'clock the next morning. This was a fair example of the gambling that went on.

The stakes were high enough to do honours to the fashionable gamblers of New York, but there was never the slightest sign of excitement. At first I used to expect that surely the card table would bring forth all sorts of flashes of tropic temperament--even a shooting or stabbing affair. But the composure was always perfect. I have seen a loser pay, without so much as a regretful remark, the sum of three million and a half reis, which, though only $1050 in our money, is still a considerable sum for a labourer to lose.

Once a month a launch comes down from Iquitos in Peru, about five days' journey up the Amazon. This launch is sent out by Iquitos merchants, to supply the wants of settlers of the rubber estates on the various affluents. It is hard to estimate what suffering would result if these launches should be prevented from reaching their destinations, for the people are absolutely dependent upon them, the region being non-producing, as I have said, and the supplies very closely calculated. In Remate de Males, the superintendent, or the mayor of the town, generally owns a few head of cattle brought by steamer, and when these are consumed no meat can be had in the region but Swift's canned "Corned Beef."

Then there are the steamers from the outer world. During the rainy season, the *Mauretania* could get up to Remate de Males from the Atlantic Ocean without difficulty, though there is no heavy navigation on the upper Javary River. But steamers go up the Amazon proper several days' journey farther. You can at the present get a through steamer from Iquitos in Peru down the Amazon to New York.

These boats occasionally bring immigrants from the eastern portions of Brazil, where they have heard of the fortunes to be made in working the rubber, and who have come, just as our prospectors came into the West, hoping to take gold and their lives back with them. Besides passengers, these boats carry cattle and merchandise and transport the precious rubber back to Para and Manaos. They are welcomed enthusiastically. As soon as they are sighted, every man in town takes his Winchester down from the wall and runs into the street to empty the magazine as many times as he feels that he can afford in his exuberance of feeling at the prospect of getting mail from home and fresh food supplies.

On some occasions, marked with a red letter on the calendar, canoes may be seen coming down the Itecoahy River, decorated with leaves and burning candles galore. They are filled with enthusiasts who are setting off fireworks and shouting with delight. They are devotees of some up-river saint, who are taking this conventional way of paying the headquarters a visit.

The priest, who occupies himself with saving the hardened souls of the rubber-workers, is a worthy-looking man, who wears a dark-brown cassock, confined at the waist with a rope. He is considered the champion drinker of Remate de Males. The church is one of the neatest buildings in the town, though this may be because it is so small as to hold only about twenty-five people. It is devoid of any article of decoration, but outside is a white-washed wooden cross on whose foundation candles are burned, when there is illness in some family, or the local patron saint's influence is sought on such a problem as getting a job. The religion is, of course, Catholic, but, as in every case where isolation from the source occurs, the natives have grafted local influences into their faith, until the result is a Catholicism different from the one we know.

The administration of the town is in the hands of the superintendent, who is a Federal officer not elected by the villagers. His power is practically absolute as far as this community is concerned. Under him are a number of Government officials, all of whom are extremely well paid and whose duty seems to consist in being on hand promptly when the salaries are paid.

The chief of police is a man of very prepossessing appearance, but with a slightly discoloured nose. His appointment reminded me of that of Sir Joseph Porter, K.C.B., in *Pinafore*, who was made "ruler of the Queen's navee" in spite of a very slight acquaintance with things nautical. Our chief of police had been *chef d' orchestre* of the military band of Manaos. They found there that his bibulous habits were causing his nose to blush more and more, so he was given the position of Chief of Police of Remate de Males. It must be admitted that in his new position he has gone on developing the virtue that secured it for him, so there is no telling how high he may rise.

The police force consists of one man, and a very versatile one, as will be seen, for he is also the rank and file of the military force. I saw this remarkable official only once. At that time he was in a sad condition from over-indulgence in alcoholic beverages. There are exact statistics of comparison available for the police and military forces. The former is just two-thirds of the latter in number. Expressed in the most easily understood terms, we can put it that our versatile friend has a chief to command him when a policeman, and a coronel and lieutenant when he is a soldier. Whether there is any graft in it or not, I do not know, but money is saved by the police-military force being one man with interchangeable uniforms, and the money must go into somebody's pocket. It might be thought that when the versatile one had to appear in both capacities at once, he might be at a loss. But not a bit of it. The landing of one of the down-river steamers offers such an occasion. As soon as the gangplank is out, the policeman goes aboard with the official papers. He is welcomed, receives his fee, and disappears. Not two minutes afterwards, the military force in full uniform is seen to emerge from the same hut into which the policeman went. He appears on the scene with entire unconcern, and the rough and ready diplomacy of Remate de Males has again triumphed.

One of the reasons for the flattering (!) name of the town, "Culmination of Evils," is the great mortality of the community, which it has as a part of the great Javary district. Its inhabitants suffer from all the functional diseases found in other parts of the world, and, in addition, maladies which are typical of the region.

Among the most important of these are the paludismus, or malarial swamp-fever, the yellow-fever, popularly recognised as the black vomit, and last but not least the beri-beri, the mysterious disease which science does not yet fully understand. The paludismus is so common that it is looked upon as an unavoidable incident of the daily life. It is generally caused by the infectious bite of a mosquito, the ***Anopheles***, which is characterised by its attacking with its body almost perpendicular to the surface it has selected. It is only the female mosquito that bites. There are always fever patients on the Amazon, and the ***Anopheles***, stinging indiscriminately, transfers the malarial microbes from a fever patient to the blood of well persons. The latter are sure to be laid up within ten days with the ***sezoes***, as the fever is called here, unless a heavy dose of quinine is taken in time to check it.

The yellow fever mosquito, the ***Stygoma faciata***, seems to prefer other down-river localities, but is frequent enough to cause anxiety. They call the yellow fever the black vomit, because of this unmistakable symptom of the disease, which, when once it sets in, always means a fatal termination. The beri-beri still remains a puzzling malady from which no recoveries have yet been reported, at least not on the Amazon. On certain rivers, in the Matto Grosso province of Brazil, or in Bolivian territory, the beri-beri patients have some chance of recovery. By immediately leaving the infested district they can descend the rivers until they reach a more favourable climate near the sea-coast, or they can go to more elevated regions. But here on the Amazon, where the only avenue of escape is the river itself, throughout its length a hot-bed of disease where no change of climate occurs, the time consumed in reaching the sea-coast is too long. The cause of this disease, and its cure, are unknown. It manifests itself through paralysis of the limbs, which begins at the finger-tips and gradually extends through the system until the heart-muscles become paralysed and death occurs.

The only precautionary measures available are doses of quinine and the use of the mosquito-net, or ***mosquitero***. The latter's value as a preventive is problematical, however, for during each night one is bound to be bitten frequently, yes, hundreds of times, by the ever-present insects in spite of all.

But if we curse the mosquito, what are we to say of certain other pests that add to the miseries of life in that out-of-the-way corner of the globe, and are more persistent in their attentions than even the mosquito? In the first place, there are the ants. They are everywhere. They build their nests under the houses, in the tables, and in the cracks of the floors, and lie in ambush waiting the arrival of a victim, whom they attack from all sides. They fasten themselves on one and sometimes it takes hours of labour to extract them. Many are the breakfasts I have delayed on awaking and finding myself to be the object of their attention. It proved necessary to tie wads of cotton covered with vaseline to the fastenings of the hammock, to keep the intruders off. But they even got around this plan. As soon as the bodies of the first arrivals covered the vaseline, the rest of the troops marched across them in safety and gained access to the hammock, causing a quick evacuation on my part. Articles of food were completely destroyed by these carnivorous creatures, within a few minutes after I had placed them on the table.

I present here a list of the various species of ants known to the natives, together with the peculiarities by which they distinguish them. I collected the information from Indians on the Seringal "Floresta" on the Itecoahy River.

Aracara--the dreaded fire-ant whose sting is felt for hours.

Auhiqui--lives in the houses where it devours everything edible.

Chicitaya--its bite gives a transient fever.

Monyuarah--clears a large space in the forest for its nest.

Sauba--carries a green leaf over its head.

Tachee--a black ant whose bite gives a transient fever.

Tanajura--one inch long and edible when fried in lard.

Taxyrana--enters the houses like the *auhiqui*.

Termita--builds a typical cone-shaped nest in the dry part of the forests.

Tracoa--its bite gives no fever, but the effect is of long duration.

Tucandeira--black and an inch and a half long, with a bite not only painful but absolutely dangerous.

Tucushee--gives a transient fever.

Uca--builds large nests in the trees.

While convalescing from my first attack of swamp-fever, I had occasion to study a most remarkable species of spider which was a fellow lodger in the hut I then occupied. In size, the specimen was very respectable, being able to cover a circle of nearly six inches in diameter. This spider subsists on large insects and at times on the smaller varieties of birds, like finches, etc. Its scientific name is ***Mygale avicularia***. The natives dread it for its poisonous bite and on account of its great size and hairy body. The first time I saw the one in my hut was when it was climbing the wall in close proximity to my hammock. I got up and tried to crush it with my fist, but the spider made a lightning-quick move and stopped about five or six inches from where I hit the wall.

Several times I repeated the attack without success, the spider always succeeding in moving before it could be touched. Somewhat out of temper, I procured a hammer of large size and continued the chase until I was exhausted. When my hand grew steady again, I took my automatic pistol, used for big game, and, taking a steady aim on the fat body of the spider, I fired. But with another of the remarkably quick movements the spider landed the usual safe distance from destruction. Then I gave it up. For all I know, that animal, I can scarcely call it an insect after using a big game pistol on it, is still occupying the hut. About nine months later I was telling Captain Barnett, of the R.M.S. ***Napo*** which picked me up on the Amazon on my way home, about my ill success in hunting the spider. "Lange," he asked, "why didn't you try for him with a frying-pan?"

CHAPTER III
OTHER INCIDENTS DURING MY STAY
IN REMATE DE MALES

Remate De Males, with Nazareth and Sao Francisco, is set down in the midst of absolute wilderness. Directly behind the village is the almost impenetrable maze of tropical jungle. If with the aid of a machete one gets a minute's walk into it, he cannot find his way out except by the cackling of the hens around the houses. A dense wall of vegetation shuts in the settlement on every side. Tall palms stand above the rest of the trees; lower down is a mass of smaller but more luxuriant plants, while everywhere is the twining, tangled *lianas*, making the forest a dark labyrinth of devious ways. Here and there are patches of tropical blossoms, towering ferns, fungoid growths, or some rare and beautiful orchid whose parasitical roots have attached themselves to a tree trunk. And there is always the subdued confusion that betokens the teeming animal life.

Looking up the Itecoahy River, one can see nothing but endless forest and jungle. And the same scene continues for a distance of some eight or nine hundred miles until reaching the headwaters of the river somewhere far up in Bolivian territory. No settlements are to be found up there; a few *seringales* from seventy-five to a hundred miles apart constitute the only human habitations in this large area. So wild and desolate is this river that its length and course are only vaguely indicated even on the best Brazilian maps. It is popularly supposed that the Itecoahy takes its actual rise about two weeks' journey from its nominal head in an absolutely unexplored region.

I found the life very monotonous in Remate de Males, especially when the river began to go down. This meant the almost complete ending of communication with the outer world; news from home reached me seldom and there was no relief from the isolation. In addition, the various torments of the region are worse at this season. Sitting beside the muddy banks of the Itecoahy at sunset, when the vapours arose from the immense swamps and the sky was coloured in fantastical designs across the western horizon, was the only relief from the sweltering heat of the day, for a brief time before the night and its tortures began. Soon the chorus of a million frogs would start. At first is heard only the croaking of a few; then gradually more and more add their music until a loud penetrating throb makes the still, vapour-laden atmosphere vibrate. The sound reminded me strikingly of that which is heard when pneumatic hammers are driving home rivets through steel beams. There were other frogs whose louder and deeper-pitched tones could be distinguished through the main nocturnal song. These seemed always to be grumbling something about "*Rubberboots--Rubberboots*."

By-and-bye one would get used to the sound and it would lose attention. The water in the river floated slowly on its long journey towards the ocean, almost 2500 miles away. Large dolphins sometimes came to the surface, saluting the calm evening with a loud snort, and disappeared again with a slow, graceful movement. Almost every evening I could hear issuing from the forest a horrible roar. It came from the farthest depths and seemed as if it might well represent the mingled cries of some huge bull and a prowling jaguar that had attacked him unawares. Yet it all came, I found, from one throat, that of the howling monkey. He will sit alone for hours in a tree-top and pour forth these dreadful sounds which are well calculated to make the lonely wanderer stop and light a camp-fire for protection.

On the other hand, is heard the noise of the domestic animals of the village. Cows, calves, goats, and pigs seemed to make a habit of exercising their vocal organs thoroughly before retiring. Dogs bark at the moon; cats chase rats through openings of the palm-leaf roofs, threatening every moment to fall, pursued and pursuers, down upon the hammocks. Vampires flutter around from room to room, occasionally resting on the tops of the iron partitions, and when they halt, continuing to chirp for a while like hoarse sparrows. Occasionally there will come out of the darkness of the river a disagreeable sound as if some huge animal were gasping for its last breath before suffocating in the mud. The sound has its effect, even upon animals, coming as it does out of the black mysterious night, warning them not to venture far for fear some uncanny force may drag them to death in the dismal waters. It is the night call of the alligator.

The sweet plaintive note of a little partridge, called *inamboo*, would sometimes tremble through the air and compel me to forget the spell of unholy sounds arising from the beasts of the jungle and river. Throughout the evening this amorous bird would call to its mate, and somewhere there would be an answering call back in the woods. Many were the nights when, weak with fever, I awoke and listened to their calling and answering. Yet never did they seem to achieve the bliss of meeting, for after a brief lull the calling and answering voices would again take up their pretty song.

Slowly the days went by and, with their passing, the river fell lower and lower until the waters receded from the land itself and were confined once more to their old course in the river-bed. As the ground began to dry, the time came when the mosquitoes were particularly vicious. They multiplied by the million. Soon the village was filled with malaria, and the hypodermic needle was in full activity.

A crowd of about fifty Indians from the Curuca River had been brought to Remate de Males by launch. They belonged to the territory owned by Mons. Danon and slept outside the store-rooms of this plutocrat. Men, women, and children arranged their quarters in the soft mud until they could be taken to his rubber estate some hundred miles up the Javary River. They were still waiting to be equipped with rubber-workers' outfits when the malaria began its work among them. The poor mistreated Indians seemed to have been literally saturated with the germs, as they always slept without any protection whatever; consequently their systems offered less resistance to the disease than the ordinary Brazilian's. In four days there were only twelve persons left out of fifty-two.

During the last weeks of my stay in Remate de Males, I received an invitation to take lunch with the local Department Secretary, Professor Silveiro, an extremely hospitable and well educated Brazilian. The importance of such an invitation meant for me a radical change in appearance--an extensive alteration that could not be wrought without considerable pains. I had to have a five-months' beard shaved off, and then get into my best New York shirt, not to forget a high collar. I also considered that the occasion necessitated the impressiveness of a frock-coat, which I produced at the end of a long search among my baggage and proceeded to don after extracting a tarantula and some stray scolopendra from the sleeves and pockets. The sensation of wearing a stiff collar was novel, and not altogether welcome, since the temperature was near the 100 deg. mark. The reward for my discomfort came, however, in the shape of the best meal I ever had in the Amazon region.

During these dull days I was made happy by finding a copy of Mark Twain's *A Tramp Abroad* in a store over in Nazareth on the Peruvian side of the Javary River. I took it with me to my hammock, hailing with joy the opportunity of receiving in the wilderness something that promised a word from "God's Own Country." But before I could begin the book I had an attack of swamp-fever that laid me up four days. During one of the intermissions, when I was barely able to move around, I commenced reading Mark Twain. It did not take more than two pages of the book to make me forget all about my fever. When I got to the ninth page, I laughed as I had not laughed for months, and page 14 made me roar so athletically that I lost my balance and fell out of my hammock on the floor. I soon recovered and crept back into the hammock, but out I went when I reached page 16, and repeated the performance at pages 19, 21, and 24 until the supplementary excitement became monotonous. Whereupon I procured some rags and excelsior, made a bed underneath the hammock, and proceeded to enjoy our eminent humourist's experience in peace.

CHAPTER IV
THE JOURNEY UP THE ITECOAHY RIVER

With the subsiding of the waters came my long-desired opportunity to travel the course of the unmapped Itecoahy. In the month of June a local trader issued a notice that he was to send a launch up the river for trading purposes and to take the workers who had been sojourning in Remate de Males back to their places of employment, to commence the annual extraction of rubber. The launch was scheduled to sail on a Monday and would ascend the Itecoahy to its headwaters, or nearly so, thus passing the mouths of the Ituhy, the Branco, and Las Pedras rivers, affluents of considerable size which are nevertheless unrecorded on maps. The total length of the Branco River is over three hundred miles, and it has on its shores several large and productive *seringales*.

When on my way up the Amazon to the Brazilian frontier, I had stopped at Manaos, the capital of the State of Amazonas. There I had occasion to consult an Englishman about the Javary region. In answer to one of my inquiries, I received the following letter, which speaks for itself:

Referring to our conversation of recent date, I should wish once more to impress upon your mind the perilous nature of your journey, and I am not basing this information upon hearsay, but upon personal experience, having traversed the region in question quite recently.

Owing to certain absolutely untrue articles written by one H----, claiming to be your countryman, I am convinced that you can not rely upon the protection of the employees of this company, as having been so badly libelled by one, they are apt to forget that such articles were not at your instigation, and as is often the case the innocent may suffer for the guilty.

On the other hand, without this protection you will find yourself absolutely at the mercy of savage and cannibal Indians.

I have this day spoken to the consul here at Manaos and explained to him that, although I have no wish to deter you from your voyage, you must be considered as the only one responsible in any way for any ill that may befall you.

Finally, I hope that before disregarding this advice (which I offer you in a perfectly friendly spirit) you will carefully consider the consequences which such a voyage might produce, and, frankly speaking, I consider that your chance of bringing it to a successful termination is Nil.

Believe me to be, etc.,

J.A.M.

During the time of my journey up the river and of my stay in Remate de Males, I had seen nothing of the particular dangers mentioned in this letter. The only Indians I had seen were such as smoked long black cigars and wore pink or blue pajamas. The letter further developed an interest, started by the hints of life in the interior, which had come to me in the civilisation of Remate de Males. I was, of course, particularly desirous of finding out all I could about the wild people of the inland regions, since I could not recall that much had been written about them.

Henry W. Bates, the famous explorer who ascended the Amazon as far as Teffe, came within 120 miles of the mouth of the Javary River in the year 1858, and makes the following statement about the indigenous tribes of this region:

The only other tribe of this neighbourhood concerning which I obtained any information was the Mangeromas, whose territory embraces several hundred miles of the western banks of the river Javary, an affluent of the Solimoes, a hundred and twenty miles beyond Sao Paolo da Olivenca. These are fierce and indomitable and hostile people, like the Araras of the Madeira River. They are also cannibals. The navigation of the Javary River is rendered impossible on account of the Mangeromas lying in wait on its banks to intercept and murder all travellers.

Now to return to the letter; I thought that perhaps my English friend had overdrawn things a little in a laudable endeavour to make me more cautious. In other words, it was for me the old story over again, of learning at the cost of experience-- the story of disregarded advice, and so I went on in my confidence.

When the announcement of the launch's sailing came, I went immediately for an interview with the owner, a Brazilian named Pedro Smith, whose kindness I shall never forget. He offered me the chance of making the entire trip on his boat, but would accept no remuneration, saying that I would find conditions on the little overcrowded vessel very uncomfortable, and that the trip would not be free from actual bodily risk. When even he tried to dissuade me, I began to think more seriously of the Englishman's letter, but I told him that I had fully made up my mind to penetrate the mystery of those little known regions. I use the term "little known" in the sense that while they are well enough known to the handful of Indians and rubber-workers yet they are "terra incognita" to the outside world. The white man has not as yet traversed this Itecoahy and its affluents, although it would be a system of no little importance if located in some other country--for instance, in the United States.

My object was to study the rubber-worker at his labour, to find out the true length of the Itecoahy River, and to photograph everything worth while. I had with me all the materials and instruments necessary--at least so I thought.

The photographic outfit consisted of a Graflex camera with a shutter of high speed, which would come handy when taking animals in motion, and a large-view camera with ten dozen photographic plates and a corresponding amount of prepared paper. In view of the difficulties of travel, I had decided to develop my plates as I went along and make prints in the field, rather than run the risk of ruining them by some unlucky accident. Perhaps at the very end of the trip a quantity of undeveloped plates might be lost, and such a calamity would mean the failure of the whole journey in one of its most important particulars. Such a disastrous result was foreshadowed when a porter, loaded with my effects, clambering down the sixty-foot incline extreme low water made at Remate de Males, lost his balance in the last few feet of the descent and dropped into the water, completely ruining a whole pack of photographic supplies whose arrival from New York I had been awaiting for months. Luckily this was at the beginning of this trip and I could replace them from my general stock.

A hypodermic outfit, quinine, and a few bistouries completed my primitive medical department. Later on these proved of the greatest value. I would never think of omitting such supplies even in a case where a few pounds of extra weight are not rashly to be considered. It turned out that in the regions I penetrated, medical assistance was a thing unheard of within a radius of several hundred miles.

A Luger automatic pistol of a calibre of nine millimetres, and several hundred cartridges, were my armament, and for weeks this pistol became my only means of providing a scant food supply.

Thus equipped I was on hand early in the morning of the day of starting, anxious to see what sort of shipmates I was to have. They proved all to be *seringueiros*, bound for the upper river. Our craft was a forty-foot launch called the *Carolina*. There was a large crowd of the passengers assembled when I arrived, and they kept coming. To my amazement, it developed that one hundred and twenty souls were expected to find room on board, together with several tons of merchandise. The mystery of how the load was to be accommodated was somewhat solved, when I saw them attach a lighter to each side of the launch, and again, when some of the helpers brought up a fleet of dugouts which they proceeded to make fast by a stern hawser. But the mystery was again increased, when I was told that none of the passengers intended to occupy permanent quarters on the auxiliary fleet. As I was already taken care of, I resolved that if the problem was to worry anybody, it would be the *seringueiros*, though I realised that I would be travelling by "slow steamer" when the little old-fashioned *Carolina* should at length begin the task of fighting the five-mile current with this tagging fleet to challenge its claim to a twelve-horse-power engine.

The *seringueiros* and their families occupied every foot of space that was not reserved for merchandise. Hammocks were strung over and under each other in every direction, secured to the posts which supported the roof. Between them the rubber-coated knapsacks were suspended. On the roof was an indiscriminate mass of chicken-coops with feathered occupants; and humanity.

About midships on each lighter was a store-room, one of which was occupied by the clerk who accompanied the launch. In this they generously offered me the opportunity of making my headquarters during the trip. The room was about six feet by eight and contained a multitude of luxuries and necessities for the rubber-workers. There were .44 Winchester rifles in large numbers, the usual, indispensable Collins machete, and tobacco in six-feet-long, spindle-shaped rolls. There was also the "***" Hennessy cognac, selling at 40,000 reis ($14.00 gold) a bottle; and every variety of canned edible from California pears to Horlick's malted milk, from Armour's corned beef to Heinz's sweet pickles.

Every one was anxious to get started; I, who had more to look forward to than months of monotonous labour in the forests, not the least. At last the owner of the boat arrived, it being then two o'clock in the afternoon. He came aboard to shake hands with everyone and after a long period of talking pulled the cord leading to the steam-whistle, giving the official signal for departure. It then developed that one of the firemen was missing. Without him we could not start on our journey. The whistling was continued for fully forty minutes without any answer. Finally, the longed-for gentleman was seen emerging unsteadily from the local gin-shop with no sign of haste. He managed to crawl on board and we were off, amid much noise and firing of guns.

After a two-hours' run we stopped at a place consisting of two houses and a banana patch. Evidently the owner of this property made a side-business of supplying palm-wood as fuel for the launch. A load was carried on board and stowed beside the boiler, and we went once more on our way. I cannot say that the immediate surroundings were comfortable. There were people everywhere. They were lounging in the hammocks, or lying on the deck itself; and some were even sprawling uncomfortably on their trunks or knapsacks. A cat would have had difficulty in squeezing itself through this compact mass of men, chattering women, and crying children. But I had no sooner begun to reflect adversely on the situation, than the old charm of the Amazon asserted itself again and made me oblivious to anything so trivial as personal comfort surroundings. I became lost to myself in the enjoyment of the river.

That old fig-tree on the bank is worth looking at. The mass of its branches, once so high-reaching and ornamental, now lie on the ground in a confused huddle, shattered and covered with parasites and orchids, while millions of ants are in full activity destroying the last clusters of foliage. It is only a question of weeks, perhaps days, before some blast of wind will throw this humbled forest-monarch over the steep bank of the river. When the water rises again, the trunk with a few skeleton branches will be carried away with the current to begin a slow but relentless drift to old Father Amazon. Here and there will be a little pause, while the river gods decide, and then it will move on, to be caught somewhere along the course and contribute to the formation of some new island or complete its last long journey to the Atlantic Ocean.

As the launch rounds bend after bend in the river, the same magnificent forest scenery is repeated over and over again. Sometimes a tall matamata tree stands in a little accidental clearing, entirely covered with a luxuriant growth of vegetation. But these are borrowed plumes. Bushropes, climbers, and vines have clothed it from root to topmost branch, but they are only examples of the legion of beautiful parasites that seem to abound in the tropics. They will sap the vitality of this masterpiece of Nature, until in its turn it will fall before some stormy night's blow. All along the shore there is a myriad life among the trees and beautifully coloured birds flash in and out of the branches. You can hear a nervous chattering and discern little brown bodies swinging from branch to branch, or hanging suspended for fractions of a second from the network of climbers and aerial roots. They are monkeys. They follow the launch along the trees on the banks for a while and then disappear.

The sun is glaring down on the little craft and its human freight. The temperature is 112 degrees (F.) in the shade and the only place for possible relief is on a box of cognac alongside the commandant's hammock. He has fastened this directly behind the wheel so that he can watch the steersman, an Indian with filed teeth and a machete stuck in his belt.

Would anyone think that these trees, lining the shore for miles and miles and looking so beautiful and harmless by day, have a miasmatic breath or exhalation at night that produces a severe fever in one who is subjected for any length of time to their influence. It would be impossible for even the most fantastical scenic artist to exaggerate the picturesque combinations of colour and form ever changing like a kaleidoscope to exhibit new delights. A tall and slender palm can be seen in its simple beauty alongside the white trunk of the embauba tree, with umbrella-shaped crown, covered and gracefully draped with vines and hanging plants, whose roots drop down until they reach the water, or join and twist themselves until they form a leaf-portiere. And for thousands of square miles this ever changing display of floral splendour is repeated and repeated. And it would be a treat for an ornithologist to pass up the river. A hundred times a day flocks of small paroquets fly screaming over our heads and settle behind the trees. Large, green, blue, and scarlet parrots, the araras, fly in pairs, uttering penetrating, harsh cries, and sometimes an egret with her precious snow-white plumage would keep just ahead of us with graceful wing-motion, until she chose a spot to alight among the low bushes close to the water-front.

The dark blue toucan, with its enormous scarlet and yellow beak, would suddenly appear and fly up with peculiar jerky swoops, at the same time uttering its yelping cry. Several times I saw light green lizards of from three to four feet in length stretched out on branches of dead trees and staring at us as we passed.

Night came and drew its sombre curtain over the splendours. I was now shown a place of unpretentious dimensions where I could suspend my hammock, but, unluckily, things were so crowded that there was no room for a mosquito-net around me. Under ordinary circumstances, neglect of this would have been an inexcusable lack of prudence, but I lay down trusting that the draft created by the passage of the boat would keep the insect pests away, as they told me it would. I found that experience had taught them rightly.

To the post where I tied the foot-end of my hammock there were fastened six other hammocks. Consequently seven pairs of feet were bound to come into pretty close contact with each other. While I was lucky enough to have the hammock closest to the rail, I was unlucky enough to have as my next neighbour a woman; she was part Brazilian negro and part Indian. She had her teeth filed sharp like shark's teeth, wore brass rings in her ears, large enough to suspend portieres from, and smoked a pipe continually. I found later that it was a habit to take the pipe to bed with her, so that she could begin smoking the first thing in the morning. She used a very expensive Parisian perfume, whether to mitigate the effects of the pipe or not, I do not know.

Under the conditions I have described I lay down in my hammock, but found that sleep was impossible. There was nothing to do but resign myself to Fate and find amusement, with all the philosophy possible, by staring at the sky. I counted the stars over and over again and tried to identify old friends among the constellations. Among them the Southern Cross was a stranger to me, but the Great Dipper, one end of which was almost hidden behind the trees, I recognised with all the freedom of years of acquaintance. My mind went back to the last time I had seen it; across the house-tops of old Manhattan it was, and under what widely different conditions!

At last a merciful Providence closed my eyes and I was soon transported by the arms of Morpheus to the little lake in Central Park that I had liked so well. I dreamed of gliding slowly over the waters of that placid lake, and awoke to find myself being energetically kicked in the shins by my female neighbour. There was nothing to do but indulge in a few appropriate thoughts on this community-sleep-ing-apartment life, and then I got up to wander forward, as best I could in the dark, across the sleeping forms and take refuge on top of my case of cognac.

We seemed to be down in a pool of vast darkness, of whose walls no one could guess the limits. I listened to the gurgling of water at the bow and wondered how it was possible for the man at the wheel to guide our course without colliding with the many tree trunks that were scattered everywhere about us. The river wound back and forth, hardly ever running straight for more than half a mile, and the pilot continually had to steer the boat almost to the opposite bank to keep the trailing canoes from stranding on the sand-bars at the turns. Now and then a lightning flash would illuminate the wild banks, proving that we were not on the bosom of some Cimmerian lake, but following a continuous stream that stretched far ahead, and I could get a glimpse of the dark, doubly-mysterious forests on either hand; and now and then a huge tree-trunk would slip swiftly and silently past us.

The only interruption of the perfect quiet that prevailed was the occasional outburst of roars from the throat of the howling monkey, which I had come to know as making the night hideous in Remate de Males. But the present environment added just the proper atmosphere to make one think for a second that he was participating in some phantasm of Dante's.

There was no particular incident to record on the trip, till June the 16th, in the night-time, when we arrived at Porto Alegre, the glad harbour, which consisted of one hut. This hut belonged to the proprietor of a *seringale*. I followed the captain and the clerk ashore and, with them, was warmly received by the owner, when we had clambered up the ladder in front of the hut. He had not heard from civilisation for seven months, and was very glad to see people from the outside world, especially as they were bringing a consignment of merchandise that would enable him to commence the annual tapping of the rubber trees.

About a dozen *seringueiros* and their families disembarked here and went without ceremony to their quarters, where they had a fire going in less than no time.

It is the custom in this section of Brazil to make visitors welcome in a rather complicated manner. You first place your arm around the other man's waist, resting the palm of your hand on his back. Then with the other hand you pat him on the shoulder, or as near that point as you can reach. Whether it recalled my wrestling practice or not, I do not know, but the first time I ever tried this, I nearly succeeded in throwing down the man I was seeking to honour.

After the proprietor had greeted each of us in this cordial way, we sat down. A large negress made her appearance, smoking a pipe and carrying a tray full of tiny cups, filled with the usual unsweetened jet-black coffee. After a brief stay, during which business was discussed and an account given of the manner of death of all the friends who had departed this life during the season in Remate de Males, we took our leave and were off again, in the middle of the night, amid a general discharging of rifles and much blowing of the steam-whistle.

The night was intensely dark, what moon there was being hidden behind clouds most of the time, and an occasional flash of lightning would show us that we were running very close to the shores. I decided to go on the roof of the right-hand lighter, where I thought I would get better air and feel more comfortable than in the close quarters below. On the roof I found some old rags and a rubber coated knapsack. Taking these to the stern, I lay down upon them and went to sleep. I imagine that I must have been asleep about two hours, when I was aroused by a crashing sound that came from the forepart of the boat. Luckily, I had fallen asleep with my eyeglasses on, otherwise, as I am near-sighted, I should not have been able to grasp the situation as quickly as proved necessary.

We were so close to the shore that the branches of a low-hanging tree swept across the top of the lighter, and it was this branch that caused the turmoil as the craft passed through it, causing everything to be torn from the roof; trunks, bags, and chicken-coops, in a disordered mass. I had received no warning and hardly had collected my senses before this avalanche was upon me. Seizing the branches as they came, I held on for dear life. I tried to scramble over them to the other part of the roof, but having fallen asleep on the stern there was no chance.

I felt myself being lifted off the boat, and as I blindly held on I had time to wonder whether the tree would keep me out of the water, or lower me into the waiting jaws of some late alligator. But it did better than that for me. The branches sagged under my weight, and I soon saw that they were going to lower me upon the trailing canoes. I did not wait to choose any particular canoe, but, as the first one came beneath me, I dropped off, landing directly on top of a sleeping rubber-worker and giving him probably as bad a scare as I had had. For the remainder of the night I considered the case of cognac, previously referred to, a marvellously comfortable and safe place to stay.

During the next day we made two stops, and at the second took on board eighteen more passengers. It seemed to me that they would have to sleep in a vertical position, since, as far as I could discover, the places where it could be done horizontally were all occupied. At five in the afternoon of this day, we arrived at a small rubber estate called Boa Vista, where the owner kept cut palm-wood to be used for the launch, besides bananas, pineapples and a small patch of cocoa-plants. The firemen of our launch were busily engaged in carrying the wood, when one of them suddenly threw off his load and came running down the bank. The others scattered like frightened sheep, and only with difficulty could be brought to explain that they had seen a snake of a poisonous variety. We crept slowly up to the place under the wood-pile which they had pointed out, and there about a foot of the tail of a beautifully decorated snake was projecting. I jammed my twenty-four-inch machete through it longitudinally, at the same time jumping back, since it was impossible to judge accurately where the head might come from. It emerged suddenly about where we expected, the thin tongue working in and out with lightning speed and the reptile evidently in a state of great rage, for which I could hardly blame it, as its tail was pinned down and perforated with a machete. We dispatched it with a blow on the head and on measuring it found the length to be nearly nine feet. The interrupted loading of wood continued without much additional excitement and we were soon on our way again.

That night I passed very badly. My female neighbour insisted on using the edge of my hammock for a foot-rest, and, to add to my general discomfort, my hammock persisted in assuming a convex shape rather than a more conventional and convenient concave, which put me in constant danger of being thrown headlong into the river, only a few inches away. Finally, I took my hammock down from its fastenings and went aft where I found a vacant canoe among those still trailing behind. I threw my hammock in the bottom and with this for a bed managed to fall asleep, now and then receiving a blow from some unusually low branch which threatened to upset my floating couch.

The next morning it was found that we had lost two canoes, evidently torn loose during the night without anybody noticing the accident. Luckily, I had not chosen either of these to sleep in, nor had anyone else. I cannot help thinking what my feelings would have been if I had found myself adrift far behind the launch.

For several days more we continued going up the seemingly endless river. Human habitations were far apart, the last ones we had seen as much as eighty-five miles below. We expected soon to be in the territory owned by Coronel da Silva, the richest rubber proprietor in the Javary region. I found the level of this land we were passing through to be slightly higher than any I had traversed as yet, although even here we were passing through an entirely submerged stretch of forest. There were high inland spaces that had already begun to dry up, as we could see, and this was the main indication of higher altitude than had been found lower down the river. Another indication was that big game was more in evidence. The animals find here a good feeding place without the necessity of migrating to distant locations when the water begins to come through the forest.

At a place, with the name of Nova Aurora, again consisting of one hut, we found a quantity of skins stretched in the sunlight to dry. They were mostly the hides of yellow jaguars, or pumas, as we call them in the United States, and seven feet from the nose to the end of the tail was not an unusual length. Although, as we learned, they had been taken from the animals only a few weeks previously, they had already been partly destroyed by the gnawing of rats. A tapir, weighing nearly seven hundred and fifty pounds, had been shot the day before and was being cut up for food when we arrived. We were invited to stay and take dinner here, and I had my first opportunity of tasting roast tapir. I found that it resembled roast beef very much, only sweeter, and the enjoyment of this food belongs among the very few pleasant memories I preserve of this trip.

While they were getting dinner ready, I noticed what I took to be a stuffed parrot on a beam in the kitchen. But when I touched its tail I found that it was enough alive to come near snapping my finger off. It was a very large arara parrot with two tail feathers, each about thirty-six inches long, a magnificent specimen worthy of a place in a museum. Parrots of this particular species are very difficult to handle, being as stupid and malicious as they are beautiful. They often made me think of dandies who go resplendent in fine clothes but are less conspicuous for mental excellences.

After having indulged in black coffee, we were invited to give the house and the surroundings a general inspection. Directly behind the structure was the smoking hut, or ***defumador***, as it is called. Inside this are a number of sticks inclined in pyramid form and covered with palm-leaves. In the floor a hole was dug for the fire that serves for coagulating the rubber-milk. Over this pit is hung a sort of frame for guiding the heavy stick employed in the smoking of the rubber. At this time the process had not become for me the familiar story that it was destined to be. Beneath the hut were several unfinished paddles and a canoe under construction. The latter are invariably of the "dugout" type. A shape is roughly cut from a tree-trunk and then a fire is built in the centre and kept burning in the selected places until the trunk is well hollowed out. It is then finished off by hand. Paddles are formed from the buttresses which radiate from the base of the matamata tree, forming thin but very strong spurs. They are easily cut into the desired shape by the men and receive decorations from the hands of the women who often produce striking colour effects. A beautiful scarlet tint is obtained from the fruit of the urueu plant, and the genipapa produces a deep rich-black colour. These dyes are remarkably glossy, and they are waterproof and very stable.

After sunset the launch was off again. Everything went quietly until midnight, when we were awakened with great suddenness. The launch had collided with a huge log that came floating down the stream. It wedged itself between the side of the boat and the lighter and it required much labour to get ourselves loose from it. After we got free, the log tore two of the canoes from their fastenings and they drifted off; but the loss was not discovered until the next morning, when we were about thirty-five miles from the scene of the accident.

Two more days passed without any incident of a more interesting nature than was afforded by occasional stops at lonely ***barracaos*** where merchandise was unloaded and fuel for the engine taken in. We were always most cordially received by the people and invited to take coffee, while murmurs of "***Esta casa e a suas ordenes***"--This house is at your disposal--followed our departure. Unlike many conventional phrases of politeness, I do not know that the sentiment was entirely exaggerated, It is typical of the Brazilian and is to be reckoned with his other good qualities. They always combine a respect for those things that are foreign, with their decided patriotism. The hospitality the stranger receives at their hands is nothing short of marvellous, and no greater insult can be inflicted than to offer to pay for accommodations. I find any retrospective glance over the days I spent among these people coloured with much pleasure when I review incidents connected with my contact with them. There is a word in the Portuguese language which holds a world of meaning for anyone who has been in that land so richly bestowed with the blessings of Nature, Brazil. It is *saudades*, a word that arouses only the sweetest and tenderest of memories.

There were seven more days of travel before we reached the headquarters of Floresta, the largest rubber-estate in the Javary region. It covers an area somewhat larger than Long Island. Coronel da Silva, the owner, lives in what would be called an unpretentious house in any other place but the Amazon. Here it represents the highest achievement of architecture and modern comfort. It is built on sixteen-foot poles and stands on the outskirts of a half-cleared space which contains also six smaller buildings scattered around. The house had seven medium-sized rooms, equipped with modern furniture of an inexpensive grade. There was also an office which, considering that it was located about 2900 miles from civilisation, could be almost called up-to-date. I remember, for instance, that a clock from New Haven had found its way here. In charge of the office was a secretary, a Mr. da Marinha, who was a man of considerable education and who had graduated in the Federal capital. Several years of health-racking existence in the swamps had made him a nervous and indolent man, upon whose face a smile was never seen. The launch stopped here twenty-four hours, unloading several tons of merchandise, to replenish the store-house close to the river front. I took advantage of the wait to converse with Coronel da Silva. He invited me cordially to stop at his house and spend the summer watching the rubber-work and hunting the game that these forests contained. It was finally proposed that I go with the launch up to the Branco River, only two days' journey distant, and that on its return I should disembark and stay as long as I wished. To this I gladly assented. We departed in the evening bound for the Branco River. On this trip I had my first attack of fever. I had no warning of the approaching danger until a chill suddenly came over me on the first day out from Floresta. I had felt a peculiar drowsiness for several days, but had paid little attention to it as one generally feels drowsy and tired in the oppressive heat and humidity. When to this was added a second chill that shook me from head to foot with such violence that I thought my last hour had come, I knew I was in for my first experience of the dreaded Javary fever. There was nothing to do but to take copious doses of quinine and keep still in my hammock close to the rail of the boat. The fever soon got strong hold of me and I alternated between shivering with cold and burning with a temperature that reached 104 and 105 degrees. Towards midnight it abated somewhat, but left me so nearly exhausted that I was hardly able to raise my head to see where we were going. Our boat kept close to the bank so as to get all possible advantage of the eddying currents.

I was at length aroused from a feverish slumber by being flung suddenly to the deck of the launch with a violent shock, while men and women shouted in excitement that the craft would surely turn over. We were careened at a dangerous angle when I awoke and in my reduced condition it was not difficult to imagine that a capsize was to be the result. But with a ripping, rending sound the launch suddenly righted itself. It developed that we had had a more serious encounter with a protruding branch than in any of the previous collisions. This one had caught on the very upright to which my hammock was secured. The stanchion in this case was iron and its failure to give way had caused the boat to tilt. Finally the iron bent to an S shape and the branch slipped off after tearing the post from its upper fastenings. It was a narrow escape from a calamity, but the additional excitement aggravated my fever and I went from bad to worse. Therefore it was found advisable, when we arrived, late the next day, at the mouth of the Branco, to put me ashore to stay in the hut of the manager of the rubber estate, so that I might not cause the crew and the passengers of the launch inconvenience through my sickness and perhaps ultimate death. I was carried up to the hut and placed in a hammock where I was given a heavy dose of quinine. I dimly remember hearing the farewell-toot of the launch as she left for the down-river trip, and there I was alone in a strange place among people of whose language I understood very little. In the afternoon a young boy was placed in a hammock next to mine, and soon after they brought in a big, heavy Brazilian negro, whom they put on the other side. Like me they were suffering from Javary fever and kept moaning all through the afternoon in their pain, but all three of us were too sick to pay any attention to each other. That night my fever abated a trifle and I could hear the big fellow raving in delirium about snakes and lizards, which he imagined he saw. When the sun rose at six the next morning he was dead. The boy expired during the afternoon.

It was torture to lie under the mosquito-net with the fever pulsing through my veins and keeping my blood at a high temperature, but I dared not venture out, even if I had possessed the strength to do so, for fear of the mosquitoes and the sand-flies which buzzed outside in legions. For several days I remained thus and then began to mend a little. Whether it was because of the greater vitality of the white race or because I had not absorbed a fatal dose, I do not know, but I improved. When I felt well enough, I got up and arranged with the rubber-estate manager to give me two Indians to paddle me and my baggage down to Floresta. I wanted to get down there where I could have better accommodations before I should become sick again.

CHAPTER V
FLORESTA: LIFE AMONG THE RUBBER-WORKERS

It was half past five in the morning when we arrived at the landing of the Floresta estate. Since it was too early to go up to the house I placed my trunk on the bank and sat admiring the surrounding landscape, partly enveloped in the mist that always hangs over these damp forests until sunrise. The sun was just beginning to colour the eastern sky with faint warm tints. Before me was the placid surface of the Itecoahy, which seemed as though nothing but my Indian's paddles had disturbed it for a century. Just here the river made a wide turn and on the sand-bar that was formed a few large freshwater turtles could be seen moving slowly around. The banks were high and steep, and it appeared incredible that the flood could rise so high that it would inundate the surrounding country and stand ten or twelve feet above the roots of the trees--a rise that represented about sixty-seven feet in all.

When I turned around I saw the half-cleared space in front of me stretching over a square mile of ground. To the right was Coronel da Silva's house, already described, and all about, the humbler *barracaos* or huts of the rubber-workers. In the clearing, palm-trees and guava brush formed a fairly thick covering for the ground, but compared with the surrounding impenetrable jungle the little open space deserved its title of "clearing." A few cows formed a rare sight as they wandered around nibbling at the sparse and sickly growth of grass.

By-and-bye the sun was fully up; but even then it could not fully disperse the mists that hung over the landscape. The birds were waking and their calls filled the air. The amorous notes of the inamboo were repeated and answered from far off by its mate, and the melancholy song of the wacurao piped musically out from the vastness of the forest. Small green paroquets flew about and filled the air with their not altogether pleasant voices. These are the same birds that are well-known to the residents of New York and other large cities, where a dozen of them can often be seen in charge of an intrepid Italian, who has them trained to pick cards out of a box for anyone desiring his fortune told for the sum of five cents. Here they must provide by their own efforts for their own futures, however. Even at this hour the howling monkey had not left off disturbing the peace with its hideous din.

Gradually the camp woke up to the day's work. A tall pajama-clad man spied me and was the first to come over. He was a very serious-looking gentleman and with his full-bearded face looked not unlike the artist's conception of the Saviour. He bade me welcome in the usual generous terms of the Brazilians and invited me into the house, where I again met Coronel da Silva. This first-mentioned grave-looking man was Mr. da Marinha. The kindness with which he welcomed me was most grateful; especially so in my present physical condition. I noticed what had not been so apparent on my first meeting with him, that recent and continuous ravages of fevers and spleen troubles had reduced him, though a fairly young man, to the usual nerve-worn type that the white man seems bound to become after any long stay in the upper Amazon region.

Not knowing where I might stop when I left Remate de Males, I had brought with me a case of canned goods. I only succeeded in insulting the Coronel when I mentioned this. He gave me his best room and sent for a new hammock for me. Such attentions to a stranger, who came without even a letter of introduction, are typical of Brazilian hospitality.

After a plentiful meal, consisting of fried fish and roast loin of tapir, which tasted very good, we drank black coffee and conversed as well as my limited knowledge of the Portuguese language permitted. After this, naturally, feeling very tired from my travels and the heat of the day, I arranged my future room, strung my hammock, and slept until a servant announced that supper was served. This meal consisted of jerked beef, farinha, rice, black beans, turtle soup, and the national Goiabada marmalade. The cook, who was nothing but a sick rubber-worker, had spoiled the principal part of the meal by disregarding the juices of the meat, and cooking it without salt, besides mixing the inevitable farinha with everything. But it was a part of the custom of the country and could not be helped. ***De gustibus non est disputandum.***

When this meal was over, I was invited to go with the secretary, Mr. da Marinha, the man who had first greeted me in the morning, to see a sick person. At some distance from the house was a small barracao, where we were received by a *seringueiro* named Marques. This remarkable man was destined to figure prominently in experiences that I had to undergo later. He pulled aside a large mosquito-net which guarded the entrance of the inner room of this hut. In the hammock we found a middle-aged woman; a native of Ceara. Her face was not unattractive but terribly emaciated, and she was evidently very sick. She showed us an arm bound up in rags, and the part exposed was wasted and dark red. It was explained that three weeks before, an accident had forced a wooden splinter into her thumb and she had neglected the inflammation that followed. I asked her to undo the wrappings, a thing which I should never have done, and the sight we saw was most discouraging. The hand was swollen until it would not have been recognised as a hand, and there was an immense lesion extending from the palm to the middle of the forearm. The latter was in a terrible condition, the flesh having been eaten away to the bone. It was plainly a case of gangrene of a particularly vicious character.

Suddenly it dawned upon me that they all took me for a doctor; and the questions they asked as to what should be done, plainly indicated that they looked to me for assistance. I explained that I had no knowledge of surgery, but that in spite of this I was sure that if something were not done immediately the woman would have little time to live.

I asked if there was not a doctor that could be reached within a few days' journey. We discussed sending the woman to Remate de Males by canoe, but this idea was abandoned, for the journey even undertaken by the most skilful paddlers could not be made in less than eighteen days, and by that time the gangrene would surely have killed the patient.

Coronel da Silva was called in. He said that the woman was the wife of the chief of the *caucheros* and that her life must be saved if possible. I explained my own incapacity in this field once more, but insisted that we would be justified in undertaking an amputation as the only chance of preventing her death.

I now found myself in a terrible position. The operation is a very difficult one even in the hands of a skilful surgeon, and here I was called to perform it with hardly an elementary knowledge of the science and not even adequate instruments. At the same time, it seemed moral cowardice to avoid it, since evidently I was the one best qualified, and the woman would die in agony if not soon relieved. I trembled all over when I concluded that there was no escape. We went to the room and got the bistoury and the forceps given me by a medical friend before I left home. Besides these, I took some corrosive sublimate, intended for the preparation of animal skins, and some photographic clips. The secretary, after a search produced an old and rusty hacksaw as the only instrument the estate could furnish. This we cleaned as carefully as possible with cloths and then immersed it in a solution of sublimate. Before going to the patient's hut I asked the owner and the woman's husband if they were reconciled to my attempt and would not hold me responsible in case of her death. They answered that, as the woman was otherwise going to die, we were entirely right in doing whatever we could. I found the patient placidly smoking a pipe, her injured arm over the edge of the hammock. By this time she understood that she was to have her arm amputated by a surgical novice. She seemed not to be greatly concerned over the matter, and went on smoking her pipe while we made the arrangements. We placed her on the floor and told her to lie still. We adjusted some rubber cloth under the dead arm. Her husband and three children stood watching with expressionless faces. Two monkeys, tied to a board in a corner were playing and fighting together. A large parrot was making discursive comment on the whole affair, while a little lame dog seemed to be the most interested spectator. The secretary took the bistoury from the bowl containing the sublimate and handed it to me with a bow. With a piece of cotton I washed the intended spot of operation and traced a line with a pencil on the arm.

Imagine with what emotions I worked! After we had once started, however, we forgot everything except the success of our operation. I omit a description of the details, as they might prove too gruesome. The woman fainted from shock just before we touched the bone,--Nature thus supplying an effective, if rude, anaesthetic. We had forgotten about sewing together the flesh, and when we came to this a boy was dispatched to the owner's house for a package of stout needles. These were held in the fire for a few seconds, and then immersed when cold in the sublimate before they were used to join the flesh. By the time it was done, I was, myself, feeling very sick. Finally I could stand the little room of torture no longer, and left the secretary dressing the wound. Would she recover from the barbaric operation? This question kept coursing through my head as I vainly tried for a long time to go to sleep.

The next day, after an early observation of my patient, who seemed to have recovered from the shock and thus gave at least this hope of success, I spent my time going around to visit the homes of the *seringueiros*. They were all as polite as their chief, and after exchanging the salute of "Boa dia," they would invite me to climb up the ladder and enter the hut. Here they would invariably offer me a cup of strong coffee. There were always two or three hammocks, of which I was given the one I liked best. The huts generally consist of two rooms with a few biscuit-boxes as chairs, and Winchester rifles and some fancy-painted paddles to complete the furniture.

The following day I arose with the sun and, after some coffee, asked a huge small-pox-scarred fellow to accompany me on my first excursion into the real jungle. Up to this time I had only seen it from my back porch in Remate de Males and from the deck of the launch *Carolina*, but now I was in the heart of the forest and would indulge in jungle trips to my heart's content. We entered through a narrow pathway called an *estrada*, whose gateway was guarded by a splendid palm-tree, like a Cerberus at the gates of dark Hades. The *estrada* led us past one hundred to one hundred and fifty rubber trees, as it wound its way over brooks and fallen trees. Each of the producing trees had its rough bark gashed with cuts to a height of ten to twelve feet all around its circumference. These marks were about an inch and a half in length. Alongside of the tree was always to be found a stick, on the end of which were a dozen or so of small tin-cups used in collecting the rubber-milk. Every worker has two *estradas* to manage, and by tapping along each one alternately he obtains the maximum of the product. This particular *estrada* was now deserted as the *seringueiro* happened to be at work on the other one under his jurisdiction.

It was in a sense agreeable to work there as the sun could not penetrate the dense foliage and the air was therefore cool. After we had walked for about an hour, my big guide complained of being tired and of feeling unwell. I told him he could go back to the camp and leave me to find my way alone. Accordingly he left me and I now had the task of carrying without assistance my large 8 x 10 view-camera, a shotgun, a revolver, and a machete.

Gradually my ear caught a terrible sound which to the uninitiated would have seemed like the roaring of a dozen lions in combat, but the dreadful notes that vibrated through the forest were only those of the howling monkey. I always had a great desire to see one of this species in the act of performing this uncanny forest-concert, therefore I left the rubber pathway after placing my camera on the ground, up against a rubber tree, and commenced following the noise, cutting my way through the underbrush. I walked and walked, but the sound seemed to remain the same distance away, and I stopped to reconnoitre.

I hesitated whether to proceed or not, fearing I might lose the way and not be able to find my camera again. The monkey was not visible at all; it fact, it was not possible to see anything, unless it was very close by, so dense was the foliage. I laid my automatic pistol on a fallen tree-trunk, and was trying to figure out the chances of getting a look at my simian friend and at the same time not losing my valuable property on the pathway, when I heard another startling sound, this time near-by. I prepared myself for whatever species of animal was due, and could feel the excitement a hunter knows when he thinks he is about to get a sight of big game. Suddenly the undergrowth parted in front of me and a herd of wild boars came trotting out. I drew a bead on the biggest of the lot and fired, letting five soft-nose bullets go through his head to make sure; the others fled, and I hastened to the spot to examine my prize more closely. It was a boar of medium size, weighing in the neighbourhood of one hundred and twenty-five pounds, and he had a fine set of tusks. He was rather vicious-looking and was doing considerable kicking before he gave up the ghost. It was impossible for me to carry him through the bush owing to the fact that I had the valuable camera and apparatus to take care of, so I made a mental note of the spot, and cut his ears off. It took four hours' search to find the camera, in spite of my belief that I had not gone far, and it was late in the afternoon when I arrived at headquarters.

The very next morning there was a good opportunity to see the smoking of rubber-milk. A ***seringueiro*** had collected his product and when I went to the smoking-hut I found him busy turning over and over a big stick, resting on two horizontal guides, built on both sides of a funnel from which a dense smoke was issuing. On the middle of the stick was a huge ball of rubber. Over this he kept pouring the milk from a tin-basin. Gradually the substance lost its liquidity and coagulated into a beautiful yellow-brown mass which was rubber in its first crude shipping state.

The funnel from which the smoke issued was about three feet high and of a conical shape. At its base was a fire of small wooden chips, which when burning gave forth an acrid smoke containing a large percentage of creosote. It is this latter substance which has the coagulating effect upon the rubber-milk. When the supply of milk was exhausted, he lifted the ball and stick off the guides and rolled it on a smooth plank to drive the moisture out of the newly-smoked rubber. Then he was through for the day. He placed the stick on two forked branches and put some green leaves over the funnel to smother the fire. On top of the leaves he put a tin-can and a chunk of clay, then filled the hole in the ground with ashes. Under this arrangement the fire would keep smouldering for twenty-four hours, to be used anew for the next repetition of the smoking process.

In the afternoon we again went out to hunt. This time I took only a 12-gauge shotgun. As we travelled through the forest I was impressed once more by the fascination of the grandly extravagant vegetation.

But there is little charm about it, nothing of the tranquillity our idyllic Catskills or even the sterner Adirondacks, create. There is no invitation to repose, no stimulus to quiet enjoyment, for the myriad life of the Amazon's jungle forest never rests. There is always some sound or some movement which is bound to stir in one the instinct of self-preservation. You have to be constantly alive to the danger of disagreeable annoyance from the pests that abound, or of actual bodily harm from animals of the reptilian order.

Were I in possession of adequate descriptive power I could picture the impression that this jungle creates upon the mind of one from the North, but now, as I once more sit in a large city with sky-scrapers towering about me, and hear the rattling noise of the elevated railway train as it rushes past, my pen fails me and I have to remove myself on the wings of thought to those remote forests, fully realising, "*Beatus ille, qui procul negotiis, ut*" etc., etc. Then I can feel again the silence and the gloom that pervade those immense and wonderful woods. The few sounds of birds and animals are, generally, of a pensive and mysterious character, and they intensify the feeling of solitude rather than impart to it a sense of life and cheerfulness. Sometimes in the midst of the noon-day stillness, a sudden yell or scream will startle one, coming from some minor fruit-eating animal, set upon by a carnivorous beast or serpent. Morning and evening, the forest resounds with the fearful roar of the howling monkeys, and it is hard, even for the stoutest heart, to maintain its buoyancy of spirit. The sense of inhospitable wilderness, which the jungle inspires, is increased tenfold by this monstrous uproar. Often in the still hours of night, a sudden crash will be heard, as some great branch or a dead tree falls to the ground. There are, besides, many sounds which are impossible to account for and which the natives are as much at a loss to explain as myself. Sometimes a strange sound is heard, like the clang of an iron bar against a hard, hollow tree; or a piercing cry rends the air. These are not repeated, and the succeeding stillness only tends to heighten the unpleasant impression which they produce on the mind.

The first thing that claimed our attention, shortly after we started, was a sound of breaking branches and falling leaves, somewhere in the distance. Through the trees I could perceive that it was a big dark-grey monkey, which we had alarmed. He was scrambling up a tall tree when I fired at him. I evidently missed, for I could see him prepare for a mighty jump to a lower tree where he would be out of sight. But in the jump he got another load of pellets, which struck him in the back. His leap fell short of the mark and he landed headlong among some bushes, kicking violently as I came up to him. As he seemed strongly built and had a rather savage expression, it did not seem wise to tackle him with bare hands, therefore, as I desired to get him alive, I ran back and procured my focussing cloth, which I tied around his head. Thus I got him safely back to the camp, where he was tied to a board and the bullets extracted from his flesh. Then his wounds, which were not serious, were bound up and he was put into a cage with a bunch of bananas and a saucer of goat's milk to cheer him up a bit.

The suddenness with which these monkey delicacies disappeared, convinced me that his complete recovery was a matter of only a short time, unless perchance some hungry rubber-worker, surreptitiously, had removed these viands while nobody was looking, for bananas and milk are things which will tempt any Amazonian from the narrow path of rectitude; but it was not so in this case. The conviction as to recovery proved right, and with the improvement of his health he displayed a cheerful and fond disposition that decided me to take him back with me to New York when I should go. I have since been informed that he belonged to the Humboldt Sika species. I watched him for several months and came to like him for the innocent tricks he never tired of playing. One night he managed to liberate himself from the tree near the hut where he was tied. He disappeared for two days, but on the third he returned, chains and all. He had doubtless found life in the jungle trees not altogether cheerful with a heavy chain secured to his waist, and he had returned reconciled to captivity and regular meals. There is at present one specimen of this kind of monkey at the Bronx Zooelogical Gardens in charge of the head keeper.

At the time of low water, the so-called *prayas* appear at the bends of the river; they grow with the accumulation of sand and mud. They are wide and often of a considerable area, and on them the alligators like to bask in the sunshine of early morning and late afternoon, and the *tartarugas*, or fresh-water turtles, lay their eggs. These eggs are laid in the months of September and October on moon-lit nights and are somewhat smaller than the ordinary hen's egg, the yolk tasting very much the same, but they are covered with a tough parchment-like shell. Here on the upper Amazon the people prepare a favourite meal by collecting these eggs and storing them for two or three weeks, when they tear open the shell and squeeze out the yolks, mixing them all up into a mush with the inevitable farinha. Few people, except native Brazilians, ever acquire a relish for this remarkable dish.

I spent a whole day waiting for the elusive alligators on one of these sand-bars, but evidently they were too wise, for they never came within camera-range. I did, however, see some tapir-tracks, leading down to the water's edge. After the long wait I grew discouraged, and chose a camping place farther up the river, where I prepared a meal consisting of turtle eggs and river water. The meal was not absolutely undisturbed, as the air was full of a species of fly that derives its principal sustenance from the bodies of various dead animals always to be found through the jungle, whose teeming life crowds out all but those fittest to survive.

I had begun my vigil before sunrise, when there are two or three hours very cool and humid. In the dry season the dew which collects is of the greatest importance to animal and plant life. For the tired and thirsty wanderer, the calyx of the beautiful scarlet orchid, which grows abundantly in this region, contains the refreshment of two or three ounces of clear, cool water. But you must look carefully into this cup of nature to see that no insects lurk in its depths to spoil the draught.

I have previously described the breakfast table of the millionaire Coronel R. da Silva, with its black beans, the dreadful farinha, the black coffee, and the handful of mutilated *bolachas* or biscuits. The only variable factor was the meat, sometimes wild hog, occasionally tapir, and very often the common green parrot or the howling monkey. At most meals the *pirarucu* fish appears, especially on Mondays when the rubber-workers have had the whole of Sunday in which to indulge in the sport of shooting this gamy two-hundred-pound fish. They carry their *pirarucu* to headquarters and courteously offer the best cuts to the Coronel, afterwards cutting the rest into long strips and leaving them to dry in the sun. Jerked beef was always to be relied upon when other supplies ran low.

There must have been some terrible mystery connected with the milk. There were twenty-one cows on the place, but never a drop of milk from them was to be had. I was always afraid to ask any questions about this deficiency for fear I might be treading on dangerous ground, but with the lack of any other explanation I ascribe it to continual sickness from which the cattle must probably suffer, in common with every other living thing here.

During the month of September, the number of patients from fever, pleurisy, and accidents, at Floresta headquarters, amounted to 82% of the population. A fever resembling typhoid resulted in several cases from drinking the river-water. The Coronel claimed that Mangeroma Indians living in the interior about 150 miles from Floresta had poisoned the creeks and affluents of the Itecoahy to take revenge upon the traders who brought the much dreaded Peruvian rubber-workers up to the Itecoahy River estates. These Peruvians are hated because they abduct the women of the indigenous tribes, when on their expeditions far into the forests where these tribes live, and consequently they are hunted down and their entrance to the region as far as possible prevented.

At this morning hour in New York (Floresta is on the same meridian as New York), thousands of toilers are entering the hot subways and legions of workers are filing into their offices and stuffy shops to take their places at the huge machinery which keeps the world in motion. At the very same hour a handful of rubber-workers are passing my house, returning from their first trip in the *estradas*, where they have been tapping the trees, and on their way to the huts and a frugal breakfast. Here in the wilds of Brazil there are no subways, no worry about the "market," nor indeed any thought for the morrow. Nature supplies the rubber trees, and the "boss" the tools to work them with; the philosophy of the rubber-worker goes no farther. A shirt, trousers, and a hat are all the dress that fashion requires, and often the worker even finds the shirt superfluous. He wears a pair of overalls, and carries slung over his shoulder his rifle and the little hatchet for tapping the trees, besides a small rubber bag in which he keeps a supply of farinha and jerked beef, should he be prevented from reaching his hut in regulation time.

The *seringueiro* is free in his movements and in his mind, he is a quick and keen observer of nature, and an expert in knowledge of the cries and calls of the animals of the forest. He knows their habits and hiding-places to perfection, and he could probably astonish the naturalist by informing him of many things he has observed that his brother scientist never has heard of. He knows the names of the trees and plants in the forest and what they can be used for, though his knowledge of them is often supplemented by superstitious imaginings. He knows the multitudinous fish of the Amazon, whether they are to be caught with a net, speared, or shot with bow and arrows, or, if the hunter is of a progressive disposition, shot with rifle ball. There are varieties that have, as yet, not been seen, classified, or identified by the scientist of to-day--I am positive of having seen several such.

The inhabitant of this region is clean in his habits and in his mind as soon as he gets away from the evil influence of civilisation--which for him is the town of Remate de Males or "Culmination of Evils." He takes a bath at least twice a day, and attends closely to the cleanliness of his wardrobe, which for that matter does not absorb any considerable amount of time. As a rule, he is industrious, but frequent attacks of fever, dysentery, liver and spleen complaints, or pneumonia make him in the end, like all living things here not native to the forests, sluggish in general, and irritable on occasion.

A little distance from the headquarters lies a beautiful lake. It is not wider than the Itecoahy itself, four hundred feet on an average, and is about five miles long. It runs parallel with the river, and has only one outlet. In the dry season this amounts to nothing more than a little rivulet across which a large fallen tree has formed a natural bridge, but in January, when the waters rise, the creek is so full that the servants of Coronel da Silva can wash the linen there. After some weeks of sojourn at Floresta, I found my way to this lake, and it was here that I was able to observe some of the largest specimens of Amazonian reptiles in their haunts, where the equatorial sun had full opportunity to develop an amazing growth of faunal and floral life.

It was a most enchanting stretch of water. I had heard of the dangers lurking beneath its surface long before I saw it, so when I arrived there one morning I was surprised to find a placid lake, set in picturesque and romantic surroundings. My first impulse was to exclaim, partly to myself, and partly to the Indian Joao who accompanied me, "Why, this is Lake Innocence," so peaceful did it appear. In fact, so much did it charm me that during the remainder of my stay at Floresta there was hardly a day some part of which I did not spend in the immediate vicinity of this lake. But it was treacherous. It was the home of six or seven old alligators and of young ones--too numerous to count; the oldest reaching a length of about seventeen feet. They would lie perfectly still under the banks, among the dead branches and snags, which made the shores generally inaccessible to boat or canoe, but when a person approached they would make their presence known by violent splashing in the water and repeated loud grunts, very much resembling those of a walrus. Then they would burrow under the soft mud and remain quiet for an hour or two. In the early forenoon, before the sun became too hot, they would sun themselves, but in the sweltering mid-day hours they remained buried in the mud, and were then very hard to rouse.

I found, on the shores of the lake, two alligator nests, formed of many twigs and branches stuck together, half in the water and half in the soft slimy mud. There they deposited their eggs, oblong tough ones; and one could always count on finding the female in the neighbourhood, should one desire to visit her. I came near stepping on one of these female alligators during a morning hunt with my camera. I was intently examining a group of eggs I found under a cluster of branches, when I was startled by a splash in the water and a loud grunt. As fast as the muddy ground would let me, I scrambled up the bank, and when I reached the top I saw the alligator swimming away from the very spot where I had been standing, its small close-set eyes fastened on me. Then it disappeared in the mud.

My next encounter occurred one forenoon, when I was sitting close to the dried-up canal which formed the outlet of the lake. It was almost mid-day. I was sitting in the shade, safe from the blazing sun, enjoying a peaceful smoke. The air was fairly vibrating with heat, causing the blood to surge through my veins. Not a sound was heard except the irritating buzz of the ever-present mosquitoes. For some time I had been aware of the slow, stealthy movement of a large body near-by, though only half consciously. The heat made me sluggish and sleepy, but suddenly I awoke to the fact that the moving thing, whatever it might be, was near me. Mechanically, I released the "safety" of my automatic pistol, and then realised that out of the reeds near me was creeping a medium-sized alligator. He was making straight for the water, and I do not know whether he was cognisant of my presence or not. He was moving steadily, advancing a few inches, stopping for a minute, then resuming the journey. I believe I was not more than five feet from the head as it emerged from the fringe of reeds. I raised my camera, secured a focus, and snapped the shutter. The click of the apparatus and perhaps my movement drew his attention. He stopped abruptly. The long jaws opened toward me, displaying an enormous expanse of pink flesh and two rows of shining teeth. I lost not a second in throwing aside the camera and jumping back to a position of relative safety, whence I fired into the open mouth of the beast. I killed him. On examining the carcass, I noticed that he had unusually large eyes, indicating that he was a young specimen.

A few days later I again went to this lake--which, from my remarks, had now come to be generally called "Lago Innocencia"--to catch fish with my Indian friend Joao. He carried a bow, four arrows with detachable heads, and a harpoon six feet long. The little boat which we found close to the outlet of the lake was pushed away from the shore, we each seized one of the peculiarly decorated paddles, and were off, looking for finny game. We paddled quietly along near the shore, now and then receiving a bump from some concealed snag which nearly upset us. It requires considerable skill to navigate one of these poorly-made dugouts, the slightest move causing a disproportionate amount of disturbance of equilibrium.

Suddenly Joao jumped up, his black eyes glowing with excitement. He motioned me to keep quiet, but it was quiet superfluous for him to do this, as I was unable to talk, or even look around, for fear the canoe might upset. He seized the harpoon, and with a powerful swing sent it into the water ahead of us, at the same time grasping the line which was attached to the end. The spear sank deep into the water, and then by the vivacity with which it danced around I could tell there was something on the end of it. As he began to pull in the line, the struggle became so violent that I crept forward on my knees in the bottom of the canoe and helped him recover the spear. Only after some strenuous balancing feats and a stiff fight by both of us, did we land our game. It was a large flat fish at least four feet square, with a long whip-shaped tail, at the base of which were two barbed bones each about three and a half inches in length. Our first act was to sever this tail with a hatchet, as it was far too active to make the fish a pleasant neighbour in close quarters. When the sting-ray, or, as the Brazilians call it, the *araya*, was dead, I cut out the two barbed bones and no longer wondered why these fish are so dreaded by those who know them. Joao told me that they attack anyone who ventures into the water, and with their sharp, barbed bones inflict a wound that in most cases proves fatal, for the bones are brittle and break off in the flesh. Superstition and carelessness are the main factors that make the wound dangerous; the people believe too much in an ever-present evil spirit which abides in all the vicious and fiendish animals of the forest and swamp. Once wounded by any of these malignant creatures, they believe there is no hope of recovery and they hardly try to survive. Besides, lack of proper care and treatment of a wound generally results in its terminating in a case of septicaemia and ultimately gangrene.

I have mentioned the *pirarucu* several times as being the largest edible fish of the Amazon. When full grown, it attains a weight of two hundred and fifty pounds. In Lake Innocence we saw this remarkable fish feeding close to the shore in shallow water, surrounded by a school of young ones. The old one was about seven feet in length and the others but recently hatched, from nine to ten inches. The Indian who pointed them out to me stood up in the bow of the canoe and, fitting one of his five-foot arrows to the bow-string, sent it through the air and into the head of the big fellow.

The bow which he used was of his own manufacture. It was about seven and a half feet long, very tough and straight, and made of Caripari wood. The shafts of the arrows were made of long straight reeds, the stalks of a certain species of wild cane. The detachable part of the arrow is a short but extremely hard piece of wood upon which is fitted an iron head with two barbs. When the point pierces the flesh this hard piece comes off, but remains attached to the shaft by a short stout cord. This allows the shaft free play so that it will not break during the struggles of the victim. Then there is a line attached to the head itself so that the hunter can handle the struggling animal or fish by means of it and of the shaft of the arrow. The whole contrivance is a marvel of ingenuity in meeting the conditions the Amazon hunter is called on to face. When the arrow struck this particular *pirarucu*, at close range, he made straight for the shore, hauling the canoe and its contents after him at considerable speed. We got tangled among the low branches and fought the fish in considerable danger of being overturned--and I should not at all care to be capsized on Lake Innocence.

Finally, we got our prize ashore. I sent the Indian to headquarters, telling him to go, as fast as he could and bring assistance so that we could get the fish home. I myself mounted guard over the carcass to see that neither the turkey buzzards nor the carnivorous mammals should destroy it. If we had left it alone for even a short time, we would have found, on our return, little to remind us of its existence. The Indian returned shortly with two men. They stuck a pole through the great gills of the *pirarucu* and in this fashion carried it to the settlement.

These waters contain great quantities of another and smaller fish known as the *piranha*, scientifically termed **Serraselmus piraya**. This is quite as much dreaded by the natives as the alligator, or even as the shark along the coast. Its ferocity seems to know no bounds. It will attack other fish and bite large pieces out of their fins and tails. Although it is not much larger than the herring it can make fatal attacks on man when in large numbers.

Mr. C.B. Brown in his work on Guiana gives the following account of this fish:

The *piranhas* in the Corentins were so abundant and were so ferocious that at times it was dangerous to go into the water to a greater depth than the knees. Even then small bodies of these hungry creatures would swim in and make a dash close to our legs, and then retreat to a short distance. They actually bit the steering paddles as they were drawn through the water astern of the boat. A tapir which I shot as it swam across the water had his nose bitten off by them whilst we were towing it to the shore. The men used to catch some of them for the sport of it, and in taking the hook from the mouth produced a wound from which the blood ran freely. On throwing them back into the water in this injured condition, they were immediately set upon and devoured by their companions. Even as one was being hauled in on the line, its comrades, seeing that it was in difficulties, attacked it at once.

I heard about these fiends but had no opportunity to witness their ferocity until one day, in crossing the river in a dugout, we wounded a wild hog that had also decided to cross at the same time and at the same place. The man with the stern paddle seized his machete as he saw the hog swimming close by the port-side of the canoe and stabbed it in the shoulder, intending to tow it ashore and have a luxurious dinner of roast hog. But his dream was never realised, for the *piranhas* which had tasted the blood, I suppose, came in large numbers and set upon the unfortunate hog. In a minute the water seemed to be boiling, so great was the activity of the little demons as they tore away pieces of the flesh until it was vanishing by inches. When we reached the other shore there was not enough left of the hog to furnish a single meal.

Later I learned that certain Indian tribes leave their dead in the river for the *piranhas* to strip the flesh from the bones. It is then customary to take the remaining skeleton and let it dry in the sun, after which it is rubbed with the juice of the *urucu* plant (the *Bixa orellana*), which produces a bright scarlet colour. Then it is hung up in the hut and the Indians consider that a token of great reverence has been thus bestowed on the deceased.

Before leaving the subject of fish, I will mention another species, smaller than the *piranha*, yet, although not as ferocious, the cause of much dread and annoyance to the natives living near the banks of the rivers. In fact, throughout the Amazon this little worm-like creature, called the *kandiroo*, is so omnipresent that a bath-house of a particular construction is necessary. The kandiroo is usually three to four inches long and one sixteenth in thickness. It belongs to the lampreys, and its particular group is the Myxinos or slime fish. Its body is coated with a peculiar mucus. It is dangerous to human beings, because when they are taking a bath in the river it will approach and with a swift powerful movement penetrate one of the natural openings of the body whence it can be removed only by a difficult and dangerous operation.

A small but hard and pointed dorsal fin acts as a barb and prevents the fish from being drawn back. While I was in Remate de Males the local doctor was called upon to remove a *kandiroo* from the urethra of a man. The man subsequently died from the hemorrhage following the operation.

Largely through the danger of the attack from this scourge, though perhaps not entirely, the natives have adopted the method of bathing in use. A plunge into the river is unheard of, and bath-houses are constructed so as to make this unnecessary. A hole about eighteen inches square is cut in the middle of the floor--built immediately above the water--through which the bather, provided with a calabash or gourd of the bread-fruit tree, dips water up and pours it over himself after he has first examined it carefully. The indigenous Indians, living in the remote parts of the forest, do not use this mode of protection, but cover the vulnerable portions of the body carefully with strips of bark, which render complete immersion less dangerous.

During my walks in the forest I often came across snakes of considerable length, but never found any difficulty in killing them, as they were sluggish in their movements and seemed to be inoffensive. The rubber-workers, who had no doubt had many encounters with reptiles, told me about large *sucurujus* or boa-constrictors, which had their homes in the river not many miles from headquarters. They told me that these snakes were in possession of hypnotic powers, but this, like many other assertions, should be taken with a large grain of salt. However, I will relate an incident which occurred while I lived at Floresta, and in which I have absolute faith, as I had the opportunity of talking to the persons involved in the affair.

Jose Perreira. a rubber-worker, had left headquarters after having delivered his weekly report on the rubber extracted, and was paddling his canoe at a good rate down the stream, expecting to reach his hut before midnight. Arriving at a recess in the banks formed by the confluence of a small creek called Igarape do Inferno, or the Creek of Hell, he thought that he heard the noise of some game, probably a deer or tapir, drinking, and he silently ran his canoe to the shore, where he fastened it to a branch, at the same time holding his rifle in readiness. Finally, as he saw nothing, he returned to the canoe and continued his way down-stream.

Hardly more than ten yards from the spot, he stopped again and listened. He heard only the distant howling of a monkey. This he was used to on his nightly trips. No! there was something else! He could not say it was a sound. It was a strange something that called him back to the bank that he had left but a few minutes before. He fastened his canoe again to the same branch and crept up to the same place, feeling very uneasy and uncomfortable, but seeing nothing that could alarm him--nothing that he could draw the bead of his rifle on. Yet, something there was! For the second time he left, without being able to account for the mysterious force that lured him to this gloomy, moon-lit place on the dark, treacherous bank. In setting out in the stream again he decided to fight off the uncanny, unexplainable feeling that had called him back, but scarcely a stone's throw from the bank he had the same desire to return,--a desire that he had never before experienced. He went again, and looked, and meditated over the thing that he did not understand.

He had not drunk **cachassa** that day and was consequently quite sober; he had not had fever for two weeks and was in good health physically as well as mentally; he had never so much indulged in the dissipations of civilisation that his nerves had been affected; he had lived all his life in these surroundings and knew no fear of man or beast. And now, this splendid type of manhood, free and unbound in his thoughts and unprejudiced by superstition, broke down completely and hid his face in his hands, sobbing like a child in a dark room afraid of ghosts. He had been called to this spot three times without knowing the cause, and now, the mysterious force attracting him, as a magnet does a piece of iron, he was unable to move. Helpless as a child he awaited his fate.

Luckily three workers from headquarters happened to pass on their way to their homes, which lay not far above the "Creek of Hell," and when they heard sobbing from the bank they called out.

The hypnotised **seringueiro** managed to state that he had three times been forced, by some strange power, to the spot where he now was, unable to get away, and that he was deadly frightened. The rubber-workers, with rifles cocked, approached in their canoe, fully prepared to meet a jaguar, but when only a few yards from their comrade they saw directly under the root where the man was sitting the head of a monstrous boa-constrictor, its eyes fastened on its prey. Though it was only a few feet from him, he had been unable to see it.

One of the men took good aim and fired, crushing the head of the snake, and breaking the spell, but the intended victim was completely played out and had to lie down in the bottom of the canoe, shivering as if with ague.

The others took pains to measure the length of the snake before leaving. It was 79 palmas or 52 feet 8 inches. In circumference it measured 11 palmas, corresponding to a diameter of 28 inches. Its mouth, they said, was two palmas or sixteen inches, but how they mean this to be understood I do not know.

This event happened while I was living at headquarters. I had a long talk with Perreira, but could not shake his statement, nor that of the three others; nevertheless, I remained a sceptic as to this alleged charming or mesmeric power of the snakes, at least so far as man is concerned.

At that time we were awaiting the arrival of the monthly launch from the town of Remate de Males, and had spent a day weighing rubber at the camp of one of the employees, half a day's journey from headquarters. The rubber-pellets were loaded into our large canoe to take up to Floresta. We spent the evening drinking black coffee and eating some large, sweet pineapples, whereafter we all took a nap lasting until midnight, when we got up to start on our night trip. It had been considered best to travel at night, when it was nice and cool with none of the pestering insects to torture us, and we were soon paddling the heavy canoe at a merry rate, smoking our pipes and singing in the still, dark night. Soon we rounded a point where the mighty trees, covered with orchids and other parasitic plants, sent their branches down to the very water which in its depths was hiding the dreaded water-snakes. The only sound we heard was the weird calling of the night-owl, the "Mother of the Moon" as the Indians call it. Except this and the lapping sound of water, as we sped along, nothing disturbed the tranquillity of the night.

I was in the act of lighting another pipe when one of the men cried out: "What's this?"

We all stopped paddling and stared ahead at a large dark object, resting on a moon-lit sand-bar not far from us. Then someone said, "*Sucuruju*." Few people can comprehend the feeling that creeps into one's heart when this word is pronounced, under such circumstances, in the far-off forest, in the middle of the night. The word means boa-constrictor, but it meant a lot more at this moment. An indescribable feeling of awe seized me. I knew now that I was to face the awful master of the swamps, the great silent monster of the river, of which so much had been said, and which so few ever meet in its lair.

Running the canoe ashore we advanced in single file. I now had a chance to inspect the object. On a soft, muddy sand-bar, half hidden by dead branches, I beheld a somewhat cone-shaped mass about seven feet in height. From the base of this came the neck and head of the snake, flat on the ground, with beady eyes staring at us as we slowly advanced and stopped. The snake was coiled, forming an enormous pile of round, scaly monstrosity, large enough to crush us all to death at once. We had stopped at a distance of about fifteen feet from him, and looked at each other. I felt as if I were spellbound, unable to move a step farther or even to think or act on my own initiative.

The snake still made no move, but in the clear moonlight I could see its body expand and contract in breathing; its yellow eyes seeming to radiate a phosphorescent light. I felt no fear, nor any inclination to retreat, yet I was now facing a beast that few men had ever succeeded in seeing. Thus we stood looking at each other, scarcely moving an eyelid, while the great silent monster looked at us. I slid my right hand down to the holster of my automatic pistol, the 9mm. Luger, and slowly removed the safety lock, at the same time staring into the faces of the men. In this manner I was less under the spell of the mesmerism of the snake, and could to some extent think and act. I wheeled around while I still held control of my faculties, and, perceiving a slight movement of the snake's coils, I fired point-blank at the head, letting go the entire chamber of soft-nose bullets. Instantly the other men woke up from their trance and in their turn fired, emptying their Winchesters into the huge head, which by this time was raised to a great height above us, loudly hissing in agony.

Our wild yelling echoed through the deep forest. The snake uncoiled itself and writhing with pain made for the water's edge. By this time we were relieved of the terrible suspense, but we took care to keep at a respectful distance from the struggling reptile and the powerful lashing of its tail, which would have killed a man with one blow.

After half an hour the struggles grew weaker, yet we hesitated to approach even when it seemed quiet and had its head and a portion of its body submerged in the water. We decided to stay through the night and wait here a day, as I was very anxious to skin the snake and take the trophy home to the States as a souvenir of a night's adventure in this far-off jungle of the Amazon. We went up in the bushes and lit a fire, suspended our hammocks to some tree-trunks, and slept soundly not more than ten yards from the dying leviathan.

We all got up before sunrise, had our coffee in haste, and ran down to see the snake. It was dead, its head practically shot to pieces. We set to work, stretching the huge body out on the sand-bar, and by eight o'clock we had the entire snake flat on the ground, ready to measure and skin.

It was a most astonishing sight, that giant snake lying there full length, while around it gathered six Amazon Indians and the one solitary New Yorker, here in the woods about as far from civilisation as it is possible to get. I proceeded to take measurements and used the span between my thumb and little finger tips as a unit, knowing that this was exactly eight inches.

Beginning at the mouth of the snake, I continued to the end and found that this unit was contained eighty-four times. Thus 84 times 8 divided by 12 gives exactly 56 feet as the total length. In circumference, the unit, the "palma," was contained 8 times and a fraction, around the thickest part of the body. From this I derived the diameter 2 feet 1 inch.

These measurements are the result of very careful work. I went from the tail to the nose over again so as to eliminate any error, and then asked the men with me also to take careful measurements in their own manner, which only confirmed the figures given above.

Then we proceeded to skin the snake, which was no easy task under the fierce sun now baking our backs. Great flocks of ***urubus***, or vultures, had smelled the carcass and were circling above our heads waiting for their share of the spoils. Each man had his section to work on, using a wooden club and his machete. The snake had been laid on its belly and it was split open, following the spinal column throughout its length, the ventral part being far too hard and unyielding. About two o'clock in the afternoon we had the work finished and the carcass was thrown into the river, where it was instantly set upon by the vigilant ***piranhas*** and alligators.

Standing in front of this immense skin I could not withhold my elation.

"Men," I said, "here am I on this the 29th day of July, 1910, standing before a snake-skin the size of which is wonderful. When I return to my people in the United States of America, and tell them that I have seen and killed a boa-constrictor nearly eighteen metres in length, they will laugh and call me a man with a bad tongue."

Whereupon my friend, the chief, rose to his full height and exclaimed in a grieved tone: "Sir, you say that your people in the north will not believe that we have snakes like this or even larger. That is an insult to Brazilians, yet you tell us that in your town Nova York there are ***barracaos*** that have thirty-five or even forty stories on top of each other! How do you expect us to believe such an improbable tale as that?"

I was in a sad plight between two realities of such mighty proportions that they could be disbelieved in localities far removed from each other.

We brought the skin to headquarters, where I prepared it with arsenical soap and boxed it for later shipment to New York. The skin measured, when dried, 54 feet 8 inches, with a width of 5 feet 1 inch.

Kind reader, if you have grown weary of my accounts of the reptilian life of the Amazon, forgive me, but such an important role does this life play in the every-day experience of the brave rubber-workers that the descriptions could not be omitted. A story of life in the Amazon jungle without them would be a deficient one, indeed.

There is a bird in the forests, before referred to, called by the Indians "*A mae da lua*," or the "Mother of the Moon." It is an owl and makes its habitation in the large, dead, hollow trees in the depths of the jungle, far away from the river front, and it will fly out of its nest only on still, moonlit nights, to pour forth its desolate and melancholy song. This consists of four notes uttered in a major key, then a short pause lasting but a few seconds, followed by another four notes in the corresponding minor key. After a little while the last two notes in the minor key will be heard and then all is still.

When the lonely wanderer on the river in a canoe, or sitting in his hammock, philosophises over the perplexing questions of life, he is assisted in his dreary analysis by the gloomy and hair-raising cry of the mother of the moon. When the first four notes strike his ear, he will listen, thinking that some human being in dire distress is somewhere out in the swamps, pitifully calling for help, but in so painful a manner that it seems as if all hope were abandoned. Still listening, he will hear the four succeeding melancholy notes, sounding as if the desolate sufferer were giving up the ghost in a last desperate effort. The final two notes, following after a brief interval, tell him that he now hears the last despairing sobs of a condemned soul. So harrowing and depressing is this song that, once heard, the memory of it alone will cause one's hair to stand on end and he will be grateful when too far away to hear again this sob of the forest.

A surprise was in store for me one day when I visited the domicile of a rubber-worker living at the extreme end of the estate. I expected to find a dwelling of the ordinary appearance, raised on poles above the ground, but instead this hut was built among the branches of a tree some twenty feet above the level of the earth. I commenced climbing the rickety ladder leading to the door of the hut. Half-way up a familiar sound reached my ear. Yes, I had surely heard that sound before, but far away from this place. When I finally entered the habitation and had exchanged greetings with the head of the family, I looked for the source of the sound. Turning round I saw a woman sitting at a ***sewing-machine***, working on a shirt evidently for her husband. I examined this machine with great curiosity and found it to be a "New Home" sewing-machine from New York. What journeys and transfers had not this apparatus undergone before it finally settled here in a tree-top in this far-off wilderness!

One afternoon while sitting in the office at headquarters discussing Amazonian politics with Coronel da Silva, Francisco, a rubber-worker, came up and talked for a while with the Coronel, who then turned to me and said: "Do you want to get the skin of a black jaguar? Francisco has just killed one on his ***estrada*** while collecting rubber-milk; he will take you down to his ***barracao***, and from there he will lead you to the spot where the jaguar lies, and there you can skin him."

I thanked Francisco for his information and went for my machete, having my pistol already in my belt. I joined him at the foot of the river bank outside the main building, where he was waiting for me in his canoe, and we paddled down-stream to his hut. On our way (he lived about two miles below Floresta) he told me that he was walking at a good rate on the narrow path of the ***estrada*** when he was attracted by a growling and snarling in the thicket. He stopped and saw a black jaguar grappling with a full-grown buck in a small opening between the trees. The jaguar had felled the buck by jumping on its back from the branches of a tree, and, with claws deeply imbedded in the neck, broke its spine and opened its throat, when Francisco drew the bead on the head or neck of the jaguar and fired. The jaguar fell, roaring with pain. Francisco was too much in a hurry to leave the narrow path of the rubber-workers and go to the spot where the victim was writhing in its death agonies, but hastened on for his dinner. Remembering later that the Coronel had offered an attractive sum of money for any large game they would bag for my benefit, and having finished his dinner, he paddled up to headquarters and reminded the Coronel of the promised reward. When we came to the hut of the rubber-worker a large dog greeted us. This dog looked like a cross between a great Dane and a Russian greyhound; it was rather powerfully built, although with a softness of movement that did not correspond with its great frame. Francisco whistled for the dog to follow us. He carried his Winchester and a machete, while I discovered that my pistol had been left unloaded when I hurried from headquarters, so I was armed with nothing but a machete. After walking for nearly half an hour, we slowed down a little and Francisco looked around at the trees and said that he thought we were on the spot where he had heard the growlings of the jaguar. It was nearing half-past five and the sun was low so we launched ourselves into the thicket towards the spot where the jaguar had been killed.

We advanced rapidly; then slower and slower. The great dog at first had been very brave, but the closer we came to the spot we were looking for, the more timid the dog became, until it uttered a fearful yell of fright, and with its tail between its legs slunk back. There was nothing to do but to leave the contemptible brute alone with its fear, so we pushed ahead. Suddenly we came to the place, but there was no jaguar. There were plenty of evidences of the struggle. The mutilated body of a beautiful marsh-deer was lying on the moist ground, pieces of fur and flesh were scattered around, and the blood had even spurted on the surrounding leaves and branches. Francisco had wounded the jaguar, no doubt--at least he said so, but plainly he had not killed it nor disabled it to such extent that it had remained on the spot.

We commenced searching in the underbrush, for it was evident it could not be far off. The bloody track could be followed for some distance; in fact, in one place the thorny roots of the remarkable *pachiuba* palm-tree, the roots that the women here use for kitchen graters, had torn off a bunch of long, beautiful hair from the sides of the jaguar, which very likely was weak and was dragging itself to some cluster of trees where it could be safe, or else to find a point of vantage to fall upon its pursuers.

We searched for some time. The forest was growing dark, and the many noises of the night began. First came the yelping of the toucan, which sounded like the carefree yap-yap of some clumsy little pup. Then came the chattering of the night monkeys and the croaking of the thousands of frogs that hide in the swamps. And still no traces of the jaguar. Again we separated. The dog had run home utterly scared. Now and then we would whistle so as not to lose track of each other. I regretted that I had been so careless as to leave my ammunition at home, as it might happen that the wounded and enraged cat would spring at us from some dark cluster of branches, and then a machete would hardly be an adequate weapon.

We searched for over an hour until it was pitch dark, but, sad to relate, we never found that jaguar. We went home silently. Francisco did not secure the reward.

This incident is of no particular interest as the result of the excursion was nil and our humour consequently very bad. But it serves to show how the mind of man will be influenced by local surroundings, and how it adapts itself to strange customs, and how a novice may be so greatly enthused that he will, half-armed, enter upon a reckless hunt for a wounded jaguar.

CHAPTER VI
THE FATAL MARCH THROUGH THE FOREST

Thus I lived among these kind and hospitable people for five months until one day my lust for further excitement broke out again, induced by a seemingly commonplace notice posted outside the door of the storeroom. It read: "The men--Marques, Freitas, Anisette, Magellaes, Jerome, and Brabo--are to make themselves ready to hunt caoutchouc in the eastern virgin forest." Puzzled as to the meaning of this, I consulted the Chief and was informed that Coronel da Silva was about to equip and send out a small expedition into the forests, far beyond the explored territory, to locate new caoutchouc trees, which were to be cut and the rubber or caoutchouc collected, whereupon the expedition was to return to headquarters with these samples and a report on the number of trees observed. This greatly interested me, and I asked the Chief, Marques, whose wife I had operated upon previously, if I could accompany him on this trip. He consented unwillingly, saying that it was very dangerous and that the same number of men that went out never came back. However, this was too rare a chance to let pass, and I made my preparations to accompany the expedition on this journey into regions where even the native *caucheros* had never before been.

On a Monday morning we all assembled at the Floresta headquarters, where Coronel da Silva bade us good-bye, and at the same time once more warned me against venturing on this trip, but I was determined and could not be persuaded to give it up.

The expedition consisted of the six men, above mentioned, all, except the Chief, Marques, unmarried. After leaving the main building we went down to the storeroom where we chose the necessary articles of food--enough to last us for three or four weeks. Our staples were to be dried *pirarucu*, the largest fish of the Amazon, some dried or "jerked" beef, and a large quantity of the farinha, the eternal woody and unpalatable meal that figures on every Brazilian's table. Besides these, we carried sugar, coffee, rice, and several bottles of "Painkiller" from Fulton Street, N.Y. Hammocks and cooking utensils completed our outfit. I took with me a large plate camera, photographic plates and paper, chemicals, scales and weights; also a magnifying glass, a primitive surgical outfit, and a hypodermic needle with several dozen prepared "ampules." My men were armed with the usual .44 Winchesters and some ancient muzzle-loaders, while I had my 9mm. automatic Luger pistol. When we were fully packed, each man carried a load weighing eighty-five pounds, strapped by means of bark strips to the shoulders, with his rifle in his left hand and a machete to clear the path in his right.

Thus equipped, we left headquarters, not knowing how or when we would see it again, while the natives fired a farewell salute, wishing us God-speed.

After a few hours by canoe, up the Itecoahy, we left the river and turned our faces inland. Our way now led through dense forest, but for four hours we travelled in a region familiar to the rubber-workers, and we were able to follow pathways used by them in their daily work.

Let no one think that a jungle trail is broad and easy. As I stumbled along the tortuous, uneven path, in the sweltering mid-day heat, pestered by legions of *pi-ums* or sand-flies and the omnipresent mosquitoes, climbing, fallen trees that impeded us at every turn, I thought that I had reached the climax of discomfort. Little could I know that during the time to come I was to look back upon this day as one of easy, delightful promenading.

The four hours' march brought us to an open place, apparently a clearing, where the *estrada* suddenly seemed to stop. Exhausted, I threw myself on the moist ground while the Chief explained our position. He said that we were now at the end of the cut *estrada* and that beyond this we would have no path to follow, though he had somewhat explored the region farther on the year previous, during a similar expedition. We found that the undergrowth had been renewed to such an extent that his old track was indistinguishable, and we had to hew our every step. When we resumed the march I received a more thorough understanding of what the word *jungle* really means. Ahead of us was one solid and apparently impenetrable wall of vegetation, but my men attacked it systematically with their heavy machetes. Slowly we advanced, but I wondered that we made any progress at all. The skill of these sons of the forest in cutting a pathway with their long knives became a constant wonder to me. Where an inexperienced person would have lost himself, looking for a round-about easy course, these men moved straight ahead, hewing and hacking right and left, the play of the swift blades seemingly dissolving all obstacles in their path. Some idea of the density of the growth can be gathered from the fact that if a man moved off he became instantly invisible although he might be only a yard or two away.

Late in the afternoon we reached a small hut or *tambo* built on the former trip by the Chief. It was nothing but a roof on poles, but it was a welcome sight to us as it meant rest and food. We were tired and hungry and were glad to find a small creek close by where we could refresh ourselves, taking care to keep out of the reach of the alligators and water-snakes swimming close to the weeds by the shore. For our supper we gave the dried *pirarucu* flesh a boil and soaked some farinha in water, eating this tasteless repast with as much gusto as we would if it had been roast beef. Let me here recommend this diet for any gourmet whose appetite has been impaired, and he will soon be able to enjoy a stew of shoe-leather. One of the men, a good-natured athlete, Jerome by name, was sent out after fresh meat, and brought back a weird little animal resembling a fox (*cuti*). We decided to test it as a stew, but, lacking salt, we found the dried *pirarucu* preferable.

The excitement of the night was furnished by ants, which had built a nest in the *tambo* where we had swung our hammocks. The visitors swarmed up poles and down ropes and would not be denied entrance. Wads of cotton smeared with vaseline and bandaged around the fastenings of the hammock proved no obstacle. It was impossible to sleep; mosquitoes came to the assistance of the ants and managed to find their way through the mosquito-net. To complete the general "cheerfulness," the tree-tops were full of little spider-monkeys whispering mournfully throughout the dark and showery night.

The second day's march took us through the region which the Chief had explored the year before, and we spent the night in another *tambo* built on that occasion. Our progress, however, was made with increasing difficulty, as the land had become more hilly and broken and the forest, if possible, more dense and wild. We were now at a considerable distance from the river-front and in a region where the yearly inundation could never reach. This stage of the journey remains among the few pleasant memories of that terrible expedition, through what I may call the gastronomic revel with which it ended. Jerome had succeeded in bringing down with his muzzle-loader a *mutum*, a bird which in flavour and appearance reminds one of a turkey, while I was so lucky as to bag a nice fat deer (marsh-deer). This happened at *tambo* No. 2. We called each successive hut by its respective number. Here we had a great culinary feast, so great that during the following days I thought of this time with a sad "*ils sont passe, ces jours de fete.*"

Now, guided by the position of the sun, we held a course due west, our ultimate destination being a far-off region where the Chief expected to find large areas covered with fine caoutchouc trees. The ground was hilly and interspersed with deeply cut creeks where we could see the ugly heads of the *jararaca* snakes pop up as if they were waiting for us. There was only one way of crossing these creeks; this was by felling a young tree across the stream for a bridge. A long slender stick was then cut and one end placed at the bottom of the creek, when each man seizing this in his right hand steadied himself over the tree to the other side of the deep treacherous water. It required steady nerve to walk this trunk, such as I did not possess, therefore I found it safer to hang from the levelled bole by my hands and travel across in that manner. *Tambo* No. 3 we constructed ourselves, as we did every other for the rest of the journey. We always selected a site near a creek that we were following, and cleared away the underbrush so as to leave an open area of about twenty-five feet square, always allowing one tree to remain for a corner. A framework of saplings tied together with strips of *matamata* bark was raised for a roof, and across this were laid gigantic leaves of the *murumuru*, twenty-five to thirty feet long. The hammocks were then strung beneath, and we managed to keep comparatively sheltered from the nightly rain that always occurs in these deep forests. After the frugal meal of *pirarucu* and dried farinha, or of some game we had picked up during the march, we would creep into our hammocks and smoke, while the men told hunting stories, or sang their monotonous, unmelodious tribal songs.

It must have been about two o'clock in the morning when I was awakened by a terrific roaring which fairly made the forest tremble. Sitting up and staring fearfully into the darkness, I heard the crashing of underbrush and trees close upon us. My first thought was of a hurricane, but in the confusion of my senses, stunned by the impact of sound, I had few clear impressions. My companions were calling one another. The noise grew louder, more terrifying. Suddenly the little world around me went to smash in one mad upheaval. The roof of the *tambo* collapsed and fell upon us. At the same instant I felt some huge body brush past me, hurling me sprawling to the ground. The noise was deafening, mingled with the shrieks and excited yellings of my men, but the object passed swiftly in the direction of the creek.

Some one now thought of striking a light to discover the extent of the damage. The *tambo* was a wreck; the hammocks were one tangled mass. Jerome, who had jumped from his hammock when he first heard the noise, followed the "hurricane" to the creek and soon solved the mystery of the storm that swept our little camp. He told us, it was a jaguar, which had sprung upon the back of a large tapir while the animal was feeding in the woods behind our *tambo*. The tapir started for the creek in the hope of knocking the jaguar off its back by rushing through the underbrush; not succeeding in this, its next hope was the water in the creek. It had chosen a straight course through our *tambo*.

The next day we were successful in killing two howling monkeys; these were greeted with loud yells of joy, as we had not been able to locate any game during the last twenty-four hours' march. This is easy to understand. We were much absorbed in cutting our way through the bushes and the game was scared away long before we could sight it.

After the ninth day of wearisome journeying, the Chief found signs of numerous caoutchouc trees, indicating a rich district, and it was accordingly decided that *tambo* No. 9 should be our last. We were now fully 150 miles from the Floresta headquarters and some 120 miles back in the absolutely unknown. That night the temperature went down to 41 deg. Fahrenheit, a remarkable drop so close to the equator and on such low ground, but it was undoubtedly due to the fact that the sun never penetrates the dark foliage of the surrounding dense forests where the swamps between the hills give off their damp exhalations.

Up to this point I had not feared the jungle more than I would have feared any other forest, but soon a dread commenced to take hold of me, now that I could see how a great danger crept closer and closer--danger of starvation and sickness. Our supplies were growing scant when we reached *tambo* No. 9, and yet we lingered, forgetful of the precarious position into which we had thrust ourselves, and the violated wilderness was preparing to take its revenge.

I suppose our carelessness in remaining was due in part to the exhausted state to which we had been reduced, and which made us all rejoice in the comfort of effortless days rather than face new exertions.

CHAPTER VII
THE FATAL "TAMBO NO. 9"

We were three weeks at *tambo* No. 9 before the sharp tooth of necessity began to rouse us to the precarious situation. Occasionally a lucky shot would bring down a *mutum* or a couple of monkeys and, on one occasion, a female tapir. Thus feasting to repletion, we failed to notice that the lucky strikes came at longer intervals; that the animals were deserting our part of the forest. During these three weeks we were not wholly idle. The Chief had the men out every day making excursions in the neighbourhood to locate the caoutchouc trees. As soon as a tree was found, they set to work bleeding the base of it to let the milky sap ooze out on the ground where it would collect in a small pool. Then they would fell the tree and cut rings in the bark at regular intervals so that the milk could flow out. In a few days when the milk had coagulated, forming large patches of caoutchouc, they would return for it. The pieces were washed in the creek and then tied into large bundles ready for transporting.

In all they located more than 800 caoutchouc trees. At this time too I made my remarkable discovery of gold deposits in the creek. It seems to me now like the plot of some old morality play, for while we were searching eagerly for the thing that we considered the ultimate goal of human desires--wealth, the final master, Death, was closing his net upon us day by day. Our food supply was nearly gone.

While strolling along the shores of the creek in search of game, I noticed irregular clumps or nodules of clay which had accumulated in large quantities in the bed of the stream, especially where branches and logs had caused whirlpools and eddies to form. They had the appearance of pebbles or stones, and were so heavy in proportion to their size that my curiosity was aroused, and throwing one of them on the bank I split it open with my machete. My weakened heart then commenced to beat violently, for what I saw looked like gold.

I took the two pieces to my working table near our **tambo**, and examining the dirty-yellow heart with my magnifying glass, I found the following: A central mass about one cubic inch in size, containing a quantity of yellowish grains measuring, say, one thirty-second of an inch in diameter, slightly adhering to each other, but separating upon pressure of the finger, and around this a thick layer of hard clay or mud of somewhat irregular shape. It immediately struck me that the yellow substance might be gold, though I could not account for the presence of it in the centre of the clay-balls.

I carefully scraped the granules out of the clay, and washing them clean, placed them on a sheet of paper to dry in the sun. By this time the attention of the other men had been attracted to what I was doing, and it seemed to amuse the brave fellows immensely to watch my painstaking efforts with the yellow stuff. I produced some fine scales I had for weighing chemicals for my photographic work, and suspended these above a gourd filled with water. Then I went down to the creek and collected more of the clay-balls and scraped the mud of one away from the solid centre of what I took to be grains of gold. A fine thread I next wound around the gold ball and this was tied to one end of the balance. After an equilibrium had been established, I found that the weight of the gold was 660 grains. Next I raised the gourd until the water reached the suspended ball, causing the opposite pan of the scales to go down. To again establish equilibrium, I had to add 35 grains. With this figure I divided the actual weight of the gold, which gave me 18.9, and this I remembered was close to the specific gravity of pure gold.

Still a little in doubt, I broke the bulb of one of my clinical thermometers and, placing the small quantity of mercury thus obtained in the bottom of a tray, I threw a few of the grains into it, and found that they immediately united, forming a dirty-grey amalgam. I was now sure the substance was gold and in less than five hours I collected enough to fill five photographic 5 x 7 plate-boxes, the only empty receptacles I could lay my hands on. I could have filled a barrel, for the creek was thick with the clay-balls as far as I could see; but I had a continuous fever and this, with the exhaustion from semi-starvation, caused me to be indifferent to this great wealth. In fact, I would have gladly given all the gold in the creek for **One** square meal. If the difficulties in reaching this infernal region were not so great, I have no doubt that a few men could soon make themselves millionaires.

The deadly fever came among us after a few days. It struck a young man called Brabo first; the next day I fell sick with another serious attack of swamp-fever, and we both took to our hammocks. For five days and nights I was delirious most of the time, listening to the mysterious noises of the forest and seeing in my dreams visions of juicy steaks, great loaves of bread, and cups of creamy coffee. In those five days the only food in the camp was howling monkey, the jerked beef and the dried farinha having given out much to my satisfaction, as I became so heartily disgusted with this unpalatable food that I preferred to starve rather than eat it again. At first I felt the lack of food keenly, but later the pain of hunger was dulled, and only a warm, drugged sensation pervaded my system. Starvation has its small mercies.

I became almost childishly interested in small things. There was a peculiar sound that came from the deep forest in the damp nights; I used to call it the "voice of the forest." To close one's eyes and listen was almost to imagine oneself near the murmuring crowd of a large city. It was the song of numerous frogs which inhabited a creek near our *tambo*. Then I would hear four musical notes uttered in a major key from the tree-tops close by, soon answered by another four in a similar pitch, and this musical and cheerful(!) conversation was continued all night long. The men told me that this was the note of a species of frog that lived in the trees.

One day the jungle took the first toll from us. Young Brabo was very low; I managed to stagger out of my hammock to give him a hypodermic injection, but he was too far gone for it to do him any good. He died in the early afternoon. We dug a grave with our machetes right behind our *tambo*. No stone marks this place; only a small wooden cross tied together with bark-strips shows where our comrade lies--a son of the forest whom the forest claimed again.

The arrival of Death in our camp showed us all how far we were in the grasp of actual, threatening danger. We stood about the grave in silence. These men, these Indians of the Amazon, were very human; somehow, I always considered them equals and not of an inferior race. We had worked together, eaten and slept and laughed together, and now together we faced the mystery of Death. The tie between us became closer; the fraternity of common flesh and blood bound us.

The next day I arose and was able to walk around, having injected my left arm with copious doses of quinine and arsenical acid. Borrowing thus false strength from drugs, I was able, to some extent, to roam around with my camera and secure photographs that I wanted to take home with me to the States.

I had constructed a table of stalks of the *murumuru* palm-leaves, and I had made a sun-dial by the aid of a compass and a stick, much to the delight of the men, who were now able to tell the hour of the day with precision. The next day I had another attack of fever and bled my arm freely with the bistoury, relieving myself of about sixteen ounces of blood. Shortly after nine o'clock in the morning I heard a shot which I recognised as being that of Jerome's muzzle-loader; soon afterward he made his appearance with a splendid specimen of a jet-black jaguar, killed by a shot behind the ear. He skinned it after first asking me if I wanted to get up and take a photograph of it, but I was too weak to do it and had to decline.

The Chief one day brought into camp a fine deer and a *mutum* bird, which relieved our hunger for a while. As we were preparing a luxurious meal, Jerome returned with two red howling monkeys, but we had all the meat we could take care of, and these monkeys were rejected and thrown away.

By this time the Chief informed us that enough caoutchouc trees had been located to justify our return to the Floresta headquarters with a satisfactory report- -of course, excepting the death of poor Brabo. Furthermore it was decided that owing to the lack of provisions we should separate. He directed that the men Freitas, Magellaes, and Anisette should take a course at a right angle to the Itecoahy, so as to reach this river in a short time, where they were to procure a canoe and secure assistance for the rest of us. This, of course, was a chance, but under the circumstances every step was a chance. The Chief himself, Jerome, and I would retrace the route which we had lately travelled and reach Floresta that way. The evening before our departure I did not think myself strong enough to carry my load a single step, but the hypodermic needle, with quinine, which had now become my constant standby, lent me an artificial strength, and when the packing was done the next morning, I stood up with the rest and strapped the load on my shoulders.

We parted with the other three men before sunrise, with clasps of the hand that were never to be repeated, and so turned our faces toward the outer world. My only hope was to retain sufficient strength in my emaciated, fever-racked body to drag myself back to Floresta, and from there, in the course of time, get canoe or launch connection to the frontier down the river, and then wait for the steamer that would take me back to "God's Country," where I could eat proper food, and rest--rest.

The jungle no longer seemed beautiful or wonderful to me, but horrible--a place of terror and death.

In my drug-dazed sleep on that back-track, I started up in my hammock, bathed in a sweat of fear from a dream; I saw myself and my companions engulfed in a sea of poisonous green, caught by living creepers that dragged us down and held us in a deadly octopus embrace. The forest was something from which I fled; it was hideous, a trap, with its impenetrable wall of vegetation, its dark shadows, and moist, treacherous ground.

I longed for the open; struggled for it, as the swimmer struggles up for air to escape from the insidious sucking of the undertow.

Starving, weak from fever, oppressed by the thought of death, but lashed on by stimulants and the tenacity of life, I headed with my two comrades out of the world of the unknown, toward the world of men--to *Life*.

CHAPTER VIII
WHAT HAPPENED IN THE FOREST

On the second day of the return trip, we had a remarkable experience. Probably not more than two hundred yards from the *tambo* where we had spent the night, we heard the noise, as we thought, of a tapir, but nothing could surpass our astonishment when we saw a human being. Who could it be that dared alone to disturb the solitude of the virgin forest, and who went along in these dreary woods humming a melody?

It was a young Indian who approached us cautiously when Jerome spoke in a tongue I did not understand, and evidently told him that we were friends on the way back to our homes by the river. He was an unusually fine specimen of a savage, well built, beautifully proportioned, and with a flawless skin like polished bronze. His clothing was limited to a bark girdle, and a feather head-dress not unlike that worn by some North American Indians.

He was armed with bow and arrows and a blow-gun; and he had a small rubber pouch filled with a brownish substance, the remarkable wourahli poison. He explained to Jerome that his tribe lived in their *maloca*, or tribal house, about 24 hours' march from this place, and that he had been chasing a tapir all day, but had lost its track, and was now returning to his home. He pointed in a north-western direction with his blow-gun, signifying thereby the general route he was going to follow in order to reach his destination. We sat down on the ground and looked at each other for quite a while, and thus I had my first chance of studying a blow-gun and the poisoned arrows, outside a museum, and in a place where it was part of a man's life. At the time I did not know that I was to have a little later a more thorough opportunity of examining this weapon. I asked the Indian, Jerome acting as interpreter, to demonstrate the use of the gun, to which he consented with a grin.

We soon heard the chattering of monkeys in the tree-tops, and deftly inserting one of the thin poisoned arrows in the ten-foot tube he pointed the weapon at a swiftly moving body among the branches, and filling his lungs with air, let go. With a slight noise, hardly perceptible, the arrow flew out and pierced the left thigh of a little monkey. Quick as lightning he inserted another arrow and caught one of the other monkeys as it was taking a tremendous leap through the air to a lower branch. The arrow struck this one in the shoulder, but it was a glancing shot and the shaft dropped to the ground. In the meantime the Indian ran after the first monkey and carried it up to me. It seemed fast asleep, suffering no agony whatever; and after five or six minutes its heart ceased beating. The other monkey landed on the branch it was aiming for in its leap, but after a short while it seemed uneasy and sniffed at everything. Finally, its hold on the branch relaxed, it dropped to the ground and was dead in a few minutes. It was a marvellous thing to behold these animals wounded but slightly, the last one only scratched, and yet dying after a few minutes as if they were falling asleep. It was then explained to me that the meat was still good to eat and that the presence of poison would not affect the consumer's stomach in the least; in fact, most of the game these Indians get is procured in this manner. I was lucky enough to secure a snap-shot of this man in the act of using his blow-gun. It proved to be the last photograph I took in the Brazilian jungles. Accidents and sickness subsequently set in, and the fight for life became too hard and all-absorbing even to think of photographing. He left us after an hour's conversation, and we resumed our journey homewards.

We had a slight advantage in retracing our former path. Although the reedy undergrowth had already choked it, we were travelling over ground that we knew, and it was also no longer necessary to delay for the building of **tambos**; we used the old ones again.

Jerome had complained for some time of a numbness in his fingers and toes, and also of an increasing weakness of the heart that made every step a torment. The Chief and I tried our best to cheer him up, although I felt certain that the brave fellow himself knew what dreadful disease had laid its spell upon him. However, we kept on walking without any words that might tend to lower our already depressed spirits.

But our march was no longer the animated travel it had been on the way out;

we talked like automatons rather than like human, thinking beings. Suffering, hunger, and drugs had dulled our senses. Only the will to escape somehow, the instinct of self-preservation, was fully awake in us. A sweep of the machete to cut a barrier bushrope or climber, one foot placed before the other, meant that much nearer to home and safety. Such was now the simple operation of our stupefied and tired brains, brains that could not hold one complex thought to its end; too tired--tired!

At nightfall we stumbled into our old *tambo* No. 7. There was no thought of securing food, no possibility of getting any; we had been too tired to even attempt to shoot game during the day. The two monkeys which the Indian had killed with his blow-gun were the only food we had and these we now broiled over the camp-fire and devoured fiercely. After this meal, none too good, we slung our hammocks with difficulty and dropped in. Jerome's numbness increased during the night. We were up and on the trail again with the dawn.

In the afternoon we descended a hill to find ourselves confronted by a swamp of unusual extent. The Chief was in the lead as we crossed the swamp and we lost him from our sight for a few minutes. While crossing this wide, slimy-bottomed place, I noticed a peculiar movement in the water near me, and soon made out the slender bodies of swamp-snakes as they whipped past among the branches and reeds. These snakes are called by the Brazilians *jararacas* and are very poisonous; however, I had no fear for myself as I wore heavy buffalo-hide boots, but the men walked barefooted, and were in great danger. I cried out a warning to Jerome, who took care to thrash about him. We supposed that we had passed this snake-hole without mishap when we rejoined the Chief on "terra firma." He was leaning over, as we approached him, and he turned a face to us that was stricken with fear. He pointed to the instep of his right foot and there on the skin were two tiny spots, marked by the fangs of the snake. Without a word we sank to the ground beside him in despair. The unfortunate man, with dilated eyes fixed upon the ground, crouched waiting for the coming of the pain that would indicate that the poison was working its deadly course, and that the end was near if something was not done immediately.

Losing no more time, I cried to Jerome to pour out some gunpowder while I sucked the wound. While doing this I fumbled in the spacious pockets of my khaki hunting-coat and secured the bistoury with which I made a deep incision in the flesh over the wound, causing the blood to flow freely. In the meantime, Jerome had filled a measure with black powder and this was now emptied into the bleeding wound and a burning match applied at once. The object of this was to cauterise the wound, a method that has been used with success in the outskirts of the world where poisonous reptiles abound and where proper antidotes cannot be had.

The Chief stood the ordeal without a murmur, never flinching even at the explosion of the gunpowder. Jerome and I made him as comfortable as possible, and sat sadly by his side watching him suffer and die by inches.

It is no easy thing to see a man meet death, but under these circumstances it was particularly distressing. The Chief had been a man of a strong constitution particularly adapted to the health-racking work of a rubber-hunter. He it was who with his forest-wisdom had planned all our moves, and had mapped our course through the blind forest, where a man could be lost as easily as on the open sea. He had proved himself a good leader, save for the fatal mistake in delaying our return, over-anxious as he was to render his employer, Coronel da Silva, full and faithful service. He was extremely capable, kind, and human, and a good friend to us all.

We had looked to him for advice in all our needs. He knew the language of the wild beasts of the forest, he knew a way out of everything, and at home he was a most devoted father. Now, this splendid fellow, the sole reliance, in this vast and intricate maze, of Jerome and myself, succumbed before our eyes to one of the dangers of the merciless wilderness. He was beyond all hope. Nothing in our power could to any extent add to the prolongation of his life which slowly ebbed away. About four o'clock in the afternoon his respirations grew difficult, and a few moments later he drew his last painful breath. He died three hours after being bitten by the *jararaca*. For the second time during that ill-fated journey I went to work digging a grave with my machete, Jerome lending me whatever assistance he could in his enfeebled state. My own condition was such that I had to rest and recover my breath with every few stabs of the machete.

We completed that day's journey late in the afternoon, arriving at *tambo* No. 6 after taking almost an hour for the last half mile. Jerome could now scarcely stand without my assistance. There was no longer any attempt to disguise the nature of his sickness. He had *beri-beri*, and that meant in our situation not the slightest chance of recovery. Even with the best of care and nursing his case would be hopeless, for in these regions the disease is absolutely fatal.

We built a fire and managed to get our hammocks fastened in some fashion, but there was not a scrap of food to be had. The heart-leaves from a young palm were chewed in a mood of hopeless desperation.

The next morning it was a task of several minutes for me to get out of the hammock and on my feet. Jerome made several painful efforts and, finally, solved his problem by dropping to the ground. He could not rise until I came to his assistance. Then we two tottering wrecks attempted to carry our heavy loads, but Jerome could not make it; he cast from him everything he owned, even the smallest personal belongings so dear to his simple, pure soul. It was heartrending to see this young man, who in health would have been able to handle three or four of his own size, now reduced to such a pitiful state.

And in my own case, the fever which I had fought off by constant use of the hypodermic needle, now swept over me with renewed violence. The drug did not have the same effect as when I was new to the ravages of the fever.

At this point my recollections became almost inextricably confused. I know that at times I raved wildly as I staggered on, for occasionally I came to myself with strange phrases on my lips addressed to no one in particular. When these lucid moments brought coherent thought, it was the jungle, the endless, all-embracing, fearful jungle, that overwhelmed my mind. No shipwrecked mariner driven to madness by long tossing on a raft at sea ever conceived such hatred and horror of his surroundings as that which now came upon me for the fresh, perpetual, monotonous green of the interminable forest.

About noon the weight on my back became unbearable and I resolved to sacrifice my precious cargo. I threw away my camera, my unexposed plates, all utensils, and four of the boxes of gold dust. This left me with one box of gold, a few boxes of exposed plates (which I eventually succeeded in carrying all the way back to New York), and fifty-six bullets, the automatic revolver, and the machete. Last, but not least, I kept the hypodermic needle and a few more ampules.

We had walked scarcely a quarter of a mile when Jerome collapsed. The poor fellow declared that he was beaten; it was no use to fight any more; he begged me to hurry the inevitable and send a bullet through his brain. The prospect of another visitation of Death aroused me from my stupor. I got him to a dry spot and found some dry leaves and branches with which I started a fire. Jerome was beyond recognising me. He lay by the fire, drawing long, wheezing breaths, and his face was horribly distorted, like that of a man in a violent fit. He babbled incessantly to himself and occasionally stared at me and broke out into shrill, dreadful laughter, that made my flesh creep.

All this overwhelmed me and sapped the little energy I had left. I threw myself on the ground some little distance from the fire, not caring if I ever rose again.

How long it was before a penetrating, weird cry aroused me from this stupor, I do not know, but when I raised my head I saw that the forest was growing dark and the fire burning low. I saw too that Jerome was trying to get on his feet, his eyes bulging from their sockets, his face crimson in colour. He was on one knee, when the thread of life snapped, and he fell headlong into the fire. I saw this as through a hazy veil and almost instantly my senses left me again.

I have no clear knowledge of what happened after this. Throughout the rest of the night, my madness mercifully left me insensible to the full appreciation of the situation and my future prospects. It was night again before I was able to arouse myself from my collapse. The fire was out, the forest dark and still, except for the weird cry of the owl, the uncanny "Mother of the Moon." Poor Jerome lay quiet among the embers. I did not have the courage, even if I had had the strength, to pull the body away, for there could be nothing left of his face by now. I looked at him once more, shuddering, and because I could not walk, I crept on all fours through the brush, without any object in mind,--just kept moving--just crept on like a sick, worthless dog.

One definite incident of the night I remember quite distinctly. It occurred during one of those moments when my senses returned for a while; when I could realise where I was and how I got there. I was crawling through the thicket making small, miserable progress, my insensible face and hands torn and scratched by spines and thorns which I did not heed, when something bumped against my thigh; I clutched at it and my hand closed around the butt of my automatic pistol. The weapon came out of its holster unconsciously, but as I felt my finger rest in the curve of the trigger, I knew that some numbed and exhausted corner of my brain had prompted me to do this thing; indeed, as I weighed the matter with what coolness I could bring to bear, it did not seem particularly wicked. With the pistol in my hand and with the safety released, I believed that the rest would have been easy and even pleasant. What did I have in my favour? What prospect did I have of escaping the jungle? None whatever--none!

There was no shadow of hope for me, and I had long ago given up believing in miracles. For eight days I had scarcely had a mouthful to eat, excepting the broiled monkey at *tambo* No. 7, shot by the young Indian. The fever had me completely in its grasp. I was left alone more than one hundred miles from human beings in absolute wilderness. I measured cynically the tenaciousness of life, measured the thread that yet held me among the number of the living, and I realised now what the fight between life and death meant to a man brought to bay. I had not the slightest doubt in my mind that this was the last of me. Surely, no man could have been brought lower or to greater extremity and live; no man ever faced a more hopeless proposition. Yet I could or would not yield, but put the pistol back where it belonged.

All night long I crawled on and on and ever on, through the underbrush, with no sense of direction whatever, and still I am sure that I did not crawl in a circle but that I covered a considerable distance. For hours I moved along at the absolute mercy of any beast of the forest that might meet me.

The damp chill of the approaching morning usual in these regions came to me with a cooling touch and restored once more to some extent my sanity. My clothes were almost stripped from my body, and smeared with mud, my hands and face were torn and my knees were a mass of bruises.

CHAPTER IX
AMONG THE CANNIBAL MANGEROMAS

I have a vague recollection of hearing the barking of dogs, of changing my crawling direction to head for the sound, and then, suddenly, seeing in front of me a sight which had the same effect as a rescuing steamer on the shipwrecked. To my confused vision it seemed that I saw many men and women and children, and a large, round house; I saw parrots fly across the open space in brilliant, flashing plumage and heard their shrill screaming. I cried aloud and fell forward when a little curly-haired dog jumped up and commenced licking my face, and then I knew no more.

When I came to I was lying in a comfortable hammock in a large, dark room. I heard the murmur of many voices and presently a man came over and looked at me. I did not understand where I was, but thought that I, finally, had gone mad. I fell asleep again. The next time I woke up I saw an old woman leaning over me and holding in her hand a gourd containing some chicken-broth which I swallowed slowly, not feeling the cravings of hunger, in fact not knowing whether I was dead or alive. The old woman had a peculiar piece of wood through her lip and looked very unreal to me, and I soon fell asleep again.

On the fifth day, so I learned later, I began to feel my senses return, my fever commenced to abate, and I was able to grasp the fact that I had crawled into the *maloca*, or communal village, of the Mangeromas. I was as weak as a kitten, and, indeed, it has been a marvel to me ever since that I succeeded at all in coming out of the Shadow. The savages, by tender care, with strengthening drinks prepared in their own primitive method, wrought the miracle, and returned to life a man who was as near death as any one could be, and not complete the transition. They fed me at regular intervals, thus checking my sickness, and when I could make out their meaning, I understood that I could stay with them as long as I desired.

Luckily I had kept my spectacles on my nose (they were the kind that fasten back of the ears) during the previous hardships, and I found these sticking in their position when I awoke. My khaki coat was on the ground under my hammock, and the first thing was to ascertain if the precious contents of its large pockets had been disturbed, but I found everything safe. The exposed plates were there in their closed boxes, the gold dust was also there and mocked me with its yellow glare, and my hypodermic outfit was intact and was used without delay, much to the astonishment of some of the men, standing around my hammock.

When my head was clear and strong enough to raise, I turned and began my first visual exploration of my immediate surroundings. The big room I found to be a colossal house, forty feet high and one hundred and fifty feet in diameter, thatched with palm-leaves and with sides formed of the stems of the **pachiuba** tree. It was the communal residence of this entire tribe, consisting, as I learned later, of two hundred and fifty-eight souls. A single door and a circular opening in the roof were the only apertures of this enormous structure. The door was very low, not more than four feet, so that it was necessary to creep on one's knees to enter the place, and this opening was closed at night, that is to say, about six o'clock, by a sliding door which fitted so snugly that I never noticed any mosquitoes or **piums** in the dark, cool room.

The next day I could get out of my hammock, though I could not stand or walk without the aid of two women, who took me over to a man I later found to be the chief of the tribe. He was well-fed, and by his elaborate dress was distinguished from the rest of the men. He had a very pleasant, good-natured smile, and almost constantly displayed a row of white, sharp-filed teeth. This smile gave me some confidence, but I very well knew that I was now living among cannibal Indians, whose reputation in this part of the Amazon is anything but flattering. I prepared for the new ordeal without any special fear--my feelings seemed by this time to have been pretty well exhausted and any appreciation of actual danger was considerably reduced as a result of the gamut of the terrors which I had run.

I addressed the Chief in the Portuguese language, which I had learned during my stay at Floresta headquarters, and also in Spanish but he only shook his head; all my efforts were useless. He let me know in a friendly manner that my hammock was to be my resting-place and that I would not be molested. His tribe was one that occupied an almost unknown region and had no connection with white men or Brazilians or people near the river. I tried in the course of the mimical conversation to make him understand that, with six companions from a big Chief's **maloca** (meaning Coronel da Silva and the Floresta headquarters), I had penetrated into the woods near this mighty Chief's **maloca**,--here I pointed at the Chief--that the men had died from fever and I was left alone and that luckily, I had found my way to the free men of the forest (here I made a sweeping movement with my hands). He nodded and the audience was over. I was led back to my hammock to dream and eat, and dream again.

Although the Chief and his men presented an appearance wholly unknown to me, yet it did not seem to distract me at the first glance, but as my faculties slowly returned to their former activity, I looked at them and found them very strange figures, indeed. Every man had two feathers inserted in the cartilage of his nose; at some distance it appeared as if they wore moustaches. Besides this, the Chief had a sort of feather-dress reaching half way down to his knees; this was simply a quantity of **mutum** feathers tied together as a girdle by means of plant-fibres. The women wore no clothing whatever, their only ornamentation being the oval wooden piece in the lower lip and fancifully arranged designs on face, arms, and body. The colours which they preferred were scarlet and black, and they procured these dyes from two plants that grew in the forest near by. They would squeeze the pulp of the fruits and apply the rich-coloured juice with their fingers, forming one scarlet ring around each eye, outside of this a black and larger ring, and, finally, two scarlet bands reaching from the temples to the chin.

There were probably sixty-five families in this communal hut, all having their little households scattered throughout the place without any separating partitions whatever. The many poles which supported the roof formed the only way of distinguishing the individual households. The men strung their hammocks between the poles in such a way that they formed a triangle, and in the middle of this a fire was always going. Here the women were doing the cooking of game that the men brought in at all times of the day. The men slept in the hammocks, while the women were treated less cavalierly; they slept with their children on the ground under the hammocks around the little family triangle. As a rule they had woven mats made of grass-fibre and coloured with the juices of the *urucu* plant and the *genipapa*, but in many instances they had skins of jaguars, and, which was more frequent, the furs of the three-toed sloths. These were placed around the family fire, directly under the hammocks occupied by the men. In these hammocks the men did most of the repair work on their bows and arrows when necessary, here they fitted the arrow heads to the shafts, in fact, they spent all their time in them when not actually hunting in the forests.

The hospitality of my friends proved unbounded. The Chief appointed two young girls to care for me, and though they were not startling from any point of view, especially when remembering their labial ornaments and their early developed abdominal hypertrophies, they were as kind as any one could have been, watching me when I tried to walk and supporting me when I became too weak. There was a certain broth they prepared, which was delicious, but there were others which were nauseating and which I had to force myself to eat. I soon learned that it was impolite to refuse any dish that was put in front of me, no matter how repugnant. One day the Chief ordered me to come over to his family triangle and have dinner with him. The meal consisted of some very tender fried fish which were really delicious; then followed three broiled parrots with fried bananas which were equally good; but then came a soup which I could not swallow. The first mouthful almost choked me,--the meat which was one of the ingredients tasted and smelled as if it had been kept for weeks, the herbs which were used were so bitter and gave out such a rank odour that my mouth puckered and the muscles of my throat refused to swallow. The Chief looked at me and frowned, and then I remembered the forest from which I had lately arrived and the starvation and the terrors; I closed my eyes and swallowed the dish, seeking what mental relief I could find in the so-called auto-suggestion.

But I had the greatest respect for the impulsive, unreasoning nature of these sons of the forest. Easily insulted, they are well-nigh implacable. This incident shows upon what a slender thread my life hung. The friends of one moment might become vindictive foes of the next.

Besides the head-Chief there were two sub-Chiefs, so that in case of sickness or death there would be always one regent. They were plainly distinguished by their dress, which consisted mainly of fancifully arranged feather belts of *arara*, *mu-*

tum, and trumpeter plumes covering the shoulders and abdomen. These articles of dress were made by young women of the tribe: women who wanted to become favourites of the Chief and sub-Chiefs. They often worked for months on a feather dress and when finished presented it to the particular Chief whose favour they desired.

The Chiefs had several wives, but the tribesmen were never allowed to take more than one. Whenever a particularly pretty girl desired to join the household of the Great Chief or of a sub-Chief, she set to work and for months and months she made necklaces of alligator teeth, peccary teeth, and finely carved ivory nuts and coloured pieces of wood. She also would weave some elaborate hammock and fringe this with the bushy tails of the squirrels and the forest-cats, and when these articles were done, she would present them to the Chief, who, in return for these favours, would bestow upon her the great honour of accepting her as a wife.

There seemed to be few maladies among these people; in fact, during the five weeks I spent with them, I never saw a case of fever nor of anything else. When a person died the body was carried far into the woods, where a fire was built, and it was cremated. The party would then leave in a hurry and never return to the same spot; they were afraid of the Spirit of the Dead. They told me that they could hear the Spirit far off in the forests at night when the moon was shining.

The men were good hunters and were experts in the use of bow and arrow and also the blow-gun, and never failed to bring home a fresh supply of game for the village. This supply was always divided equally, so that no one should receive more than he needed for the day. At first glance the men might appear lazy, but why should they hurry and worry when they have no landlord, and no grocer's bills to pay; in fact, the value of money is entirely unknown to them.

I was allowed to walk around as I pleased, everybody showing me a kindness for which I shall ever gratefully remember these "savages." I frequently spent my forenoons on a tree trunk outside the *maloca* with the Chief, who took a particular interest in my welfare. We would sit for hours and talk, he sometimes pointing at an object and giving its Indian name, which I would repeat until I got the right pronunciation. Thus, gradually instructed, and by watching the men and women as they came and went, day after day, I was able to understand some of their language and learned to answer questions fairly well. They never laughed at my mistakes, but repeated a word until I had it right.

The word of the Chief was law and no one dared appeal from the decisions of this man. In fact, there would have been nobody to appeal to, for the natives believed him vested with mysterious power which made him the ruler of men. I once had occasion to see him use the power which had been given him.

I had accompanied two young Indians, one of whom was the man we had met in the forest on our return trip not far from that fatal *tambo* No. 3. His name, at least as it sounded to me, was Rere. They carried bows and arrows and I my automatic pistol, although I had no great intention of using it. What little ammunition I had left I desired to keep for an emergency and, besides, I reasoned that I might, at some future time, be able to use the power and noise of the weapon to good advantage if I kept the Indians ignorant of them for the present.

We had scarcely gone a mile, when we discovered on the opposite side of a creek, about one hundred and fifty yards away, a wild hog rooting for food. We were on a slight elevation ourselves and under cover of the brush, while the hog was exposed to view on the next knoll. Almost simultaneously my companions fitted arrows to their bow-strings. Instead of shooting point blank, manipulating the bows with their hands and arms, they placed their great and second toes on the cords on the ground, and with their left arms gave the proper tension and inclination to the bows which were at least eight feet long. With a whirr the poisoned arrows shot forth and, while the cords still twanged, sailed gracefully through the air, describing a hyperbola, fell with a speed that made them almost invisible, and plunged into the animal on each side of his neck a little back from the base of the brain.

The hog dropped in his tracks, and I doubt if he could have lived even though the arrows had not been poisoned. Tying his feet together with plant-fibres we slung the body over a heavy pole and carried it to the *maloca*. All the way the two fellows disputed as to who was the owner of the hog, and from time to time they put the carcass on the ground to gesticulate and argue. I thought they would come to blows. When they appealed to me I declared that the arrows had sped so rapidly that my eyes could not follow them and therefore could not tell which arrow had found its mark first.

A few yards from the house my friends fell to arguing again, and a crowd collected about them, cheering first the one then the other. My suggestion that the game be divided was rejected as showing very poor judgment. Finally, the dispute grew to such proportions that the Chief sent a messenger to learn the cause of the trouble and report it to him.

The emissary retired and the crowd immediately began to disperse and the combatants quieted. The messenger soon returned saying that the Great Chief would judge the case and ordered the men to enter the *maloca*. With some difficulty the hog was dragged through the door opening and all the inhabitants crawled in after. The Chief was decked out in a new and splendid feather dress, his face had received a fresh coat of paint (in fact, the shells of the *urucu* plant with which he coloured his face and body scarlet were still lying under his hammock), and his nose was supplied with a new set of *mutum* feathers. He was sitting in his hammock which was made of fine, braided, multi-coloured grass-fibres and was fringed with numerous squirrel tails. The whole picture was one which impressed me as being weirdly fantastic and extremely picturesque, the reddish, flickering light from the fires adding a mystic colour to the scene. On the opposite side of the fire from where the Chief was sitting lay the body of the hog, and at each end of the carcass stood the two hunters, straight as saplings, gazing stolidly ahead. In a semi-circle, facing the Chief and surrounding the disputants, was the tribe, squatting on the ground. The Chief motioned to me to seat myself on the ground alongside of the hammock where he was sitting. The men told their story, now and then looking to me for an affirmative nod of the head. After having listened to the argument of the hunters for a considerable time without uttering a syllable, and regarding the crowd with a steady, unblinking expression, with a trace of a satirical smile around the corners of his mouth, which suited him admirably, the Chief finally spoke. He said, "The hog is mine.--Go!"

The matter was ended with this wise judgment, and there seemed to be no disposition to grumble or re-appeal to the great authority.

My life among the Mangeromas was, for the greater part, free from adventure, at least as compared with former experiences, and yet I was more than once within an inch of meeting death. In fact, I think that I looked more squarely in the eyes of death in that peaceful little community than ever I did out in the wilds of the jungle or in my most perilous adventures. The creek that ran near the *maloca* supplied the

Indians with what water they needed for drinking purposes. Besides this the creek gave them an abundant supply of fish, a dish that made its appearance at every meal. Whatever washing was to be done--the natives took a bath at least twice a day--was done at some distance down the creek so as not to spoil the water for drinking and culinary purposes. Whenever I was thirsty I was in the habit of stooping down at the water's edge to scoop the fluid up in my curved hands. One morning I had been tramping through the jungle with two companions who were in search of game, and I was very tired and hot when we came to a little stream which I took to be the same that ran past the *maloca*. My friends were at a short distance from me, beating their way through the underbrush, when I stooped to quench my thirst. The cool water looked to me like the very Elixir of Life. At that moment, literally speaking, I was only two inches from death. Hearing a sharp cry behind me I turned slightly to feel a rough hand upon my shoulders and found myself flung backwards on the ground.

"Poison," was the reply to my angry question. Then my friend explained, and as he talked my knees wobbled and I turned pale. It seems that the Mangeromas often poison the streams below the drinking places in order to get rid of their enemies. In the present case there had been a rumour that a party of Peruvian rubber-workers might be coming up the creek, and this is always a signal of trouble among these Indians. Although you cannot induce a Brazilian to go into the Indian settlements or *malocas*, the Peruvians are more than willing to go there, because of the chance of abducting girls. To accomplish this, a few Peruvians sneak close to the *maloca* at night, force the door, which is always bolted to keep out the Evil Spirit, but which without difficulty can be cut open, and fire a volley of shots into the hut. The Indians sleep with the blow-guns and arrows suspended from the rafters, and before they can collect their sleepy senses and procure the weapons the Peruvians, in the general confusion, have carried off some of the girls. The Mangeromas, therefore, hate the Peruvians and will go to any extreme to compass their death. The poisoning of the rivers is effected by the root of a plant that is found throughout the Amazon valley; the plant belongs to the genus *Lonchocarpus* and bears a small cluster of bluish blossoms which produce a pod about two inches in length. It is only the yellow roots that are used for poisoning the water. This is done by crushing the roots and throwing the pulp into the stream, when all animal life will be killed or driven away.

It seems strange that during my stay among the Mangeromas, who were heathens and even cannibals, I saw no signs of idolatry. They believed implicitly in a good and an evil spirit. The good spirit was too good to do them any harm and consequently they did not bother with him; but the evil spirit was more active and could be heard in the dark nights, howling and wailing far off in the forest as he searched for lonely wanderers, whom he was said to devour.

Thinking to amuse some of my friends, I one day kindled a flame by means of my magnifying glass and a few dry twigs. A group of ten or twelve Indians had gathered squatting in a circle about me, to see the wonder that I was to exhibit, but at the sight of smoke followed by flame they were badly scared and ran for the house, where they called the Chief. He arrived on the scene with his usual smile.

He asked me to show him what I had done. I applied the focussed rays of the sun to some more dry leaves and twigs and, finally, the flames broke out again. The Chief was delighted and begged me to make him a present of the magnifier. As I did not dare to refuse, I showed him how to use it and then presented it with as good grace as I could.

Some time after this, I learned that two Peruvians had been caught in a trap set for the purpose. The unfortunate men had spent a whole night in a pit, nine feet deep, and were discovered the next forenoon by a party of hunters, who immediately killed them with unpoisoned, big-game arrows. In contrast to the North-American Indians they never torture captives, but kill them as quickly as possible.

I had plenty of opportunity to investigate the different kinds of traps used by the Mangeromas for catching Peruvian *caboclos* or half-breeds. First of all in importance is the pit-trap, into which the aforesaid men had fallen. It is simple but ingenious in its arrangement. A hole about nine feet deep and eight feet wide is dug in the ground at a place where the *caboclos* are liable to come. A cover is laid across this and cleverly disguised with dead leaves and branches so as to exactly resemble the surrounding soil. This cover is constructed of branches placed parallel, and is slightly smaller than the diameter of the pit. It is balanced on a stick, tied across the middle in such a manner that the slightest weight on any part will cause it to turn over and precipitate the object into the pit whence egress is impossible. Besides this, the walls of the pit are inclined, the widest part being at the bottom, and they gradually slope inward till the level of the ground is reached. When the victim is discovered he is quickly killed, as in the case noted above.

The second trap, which I had an opportunity to investigate, is the so-called *araya* trap. It is merely a small piece of ground thickly set with the barbed bones of the sting-ray. These bones are slightly touched with wourahli poison and, concealed as they are under dead leaves, they inflict severe wounds on the bare feet of the *caboclos*, and death follows within a short period.

The third trap, and the most ingenious of all, is the blow-gun trap. One day the sub-Chief, a tall, gloomy-looking fellow, took me to one of these traps and explained everything, till I had obtained a thorough knowledge of the complicated apparatus. The blow-gun of these Indians is supplied with a wide mouth-piece and requires but slight air pressure to shoot the arrow at a considerable speed. In the trap one is placed horizontally so as to point at a right angle to the path leading to the *maloca*. At the "breech" of the gun is a young sapling, severed five feet above the ground. To this is tied a broad and straight bark-strip which, when the sapling is in its normal vertical position, completely covers the mouth-piece. The gun was not loaded on this occasion, as it had been accidentally discharged the day before. To set the trap, a long, thin, and pliable climber, which in these forests is so plentiful, is attached to the end of the severed sapling, when this is bent to its extreme position and is then led over branches, serving as pulleys, right across the path and directly in front of the mouth of the blow-gun and is tied to some small root covered with leaves. When the *caboclo* passes along this path at night to raid the Indian *maloca,* he must sever this thin bushrope or climber, thereby releasing suddenly the tension of the sapling. The bark-flap is drawn quickly up against the mouth-piece with a slap that forces sufficient air into the gun to eject the arrow. All this takes place in a fraction of a second; a slight flapping sound is heard and the arrow lodges in the skin of the unfortunate *caboclo*. He can never walk more than twenty yards, for the poison rapidly paralyses his limbs. Death follows in less than ten minutes.

The bodies of these captured *caboclos* are soon found by the "police warriors" of the tribe and carried to the *maloca*. On such occasions a day of feasting always follows and an obscure religious rite is performed.

It is true that the Mangeromas are cannibals, but at the same time their habits and morals are otherwise remarkably clean. Without their good care and excellent treatment, I have no doubt I would now be with my brave companions out in that dark, green jungle.

But to return to my story of the two Peruvians caught in the pit-trap: the warriors cut off the hands and feet of both corpses, pulled the big game arrows out of the bodies, and had an audience with the Chief. He seemed to be well satisfied, but spoke little, just nodding his head and smiling. Shortly after the village prepared for a grand feast. The fires were rebuilt, the pots and jars were cleaned, and a scene followed which to me was frightful. Had it not happened, I should always have believed this little world out in the wild forest an ideal, pure, and morally clean community. But now I could only hasten to my hammock and simulate sleep, for I well knew, from previous experience, that otherwise I would have to partake of the meal in preparation: a horrible meal of human flesh! It was enough for me to see them strip the flesh from the palms of the hands and the soles of the feet and fry these delicacies in the lard of tapir I hoped to see no more.

An awful thought coursed through my brain when I beheld the men bend eagerly over the pans to see if the meat were done. How long would it be, I said to myself, before they would forget themselves and place my own extremities in the same pots and pans. Such a possibility was not pleasant to contemplate, but as I had found the word of these Indians to be always good, I believed I was safe. They were never false and they hated falsehood. True, they were cunning, but once their friend always their friend, through thick and thin. And the Chief had promised that I should not be eaten, either fried or stewed! Therefore I slept in peace.

I had long desired to see the hunters prepare the mysterious wourahli poison, which acts so quickly and painlessly, and which allows the game killed by it to be eaten without interfering with the nutritive qualities. Only three men in this village understood the proper mixing of the ingredients, although everybody knew the two plants from which the poisonous juices were obtained. One of these is a vine that grows close to the creeks. The stem is about two inches in diameter and covered with a rough greyish bark. It yields several round fruits, shaped like an apple, containing seeds imbedded in a very bitter pulp. The other is also a vine and bears small bluish flowers, but it is only the roots of this that are used. These are crushed and steeped in water for several days. The three men in our village who understood the concoction of this poison collected the plants themselves once a month. When they returned from their expedition they set to work at once scraping the first named vine into fine shavings and mixing these in an earthen jar with the crushed pulp of the roots of the second plant. The pot is then placed over a fire and kept simmering for several hours. At this stage the shavings are removed and thrown away as useless and several large black ants, the *Tucandeiras*, are added. This is the ant whose bite is not only painful but absolutely dangerous to man. The concoction is kept boiling slowly until the next morning, when it has assumed a thick consistency of a brown colour and very bitter to the taste. The poison is then tried on some arrows and if it comes up to the standard it is placed in a small earthen jar which is covered with a piece of animal skin and it is ready for use. The arrows, which are from ten to twelve inches long, are made from the stalks of a certain palm-leaf, the Jacy palm. They are absolutely straight and true; in fact, they resemble very much a lady's hat-pin. When the gun is to be used, a piece of cotton is wound around the end of an arrow and the other end or point inserted first in the barrel, the cotton acting as a piston by means of which the air forces the shaft through the tube.

The men always carry a small rubber-pouch containing a few drams of the poison; the pouch was worn strapped to the waist on the left side, when on their hunting excursions, and they were extremely careful in handling it and the arrows. The slightest scratch with the poison would cause a quick and sure death.

I was so far recuperated by this time that I thought of returning to civilisation, and I, accordingly, broached the subject to the Chief, who answered me very kindly, promising that he would send me by the next full-moon, with some of the wourahli men, down to the Branco River, and from there they would guide me within a safe distance of the rubber-estate, situated at the junction with the Itecoahy.

One day I was informed that a friendly call on a neighbouring tribe was being contemplated and that I could accompany the Chief and his men.

At last the time arrived and the expedition was organised. I was not absolutely sure how I would be treated by these up-stream Indians, and I am almost ashamed to confess that, in spite of all the faithful, unswerving friendship which the Mangeromas had shown me, I had it in my mind that these other Indians might harm me, so black was the name that people down at the settlements had given them.

Until this time, as related above, I had thought best not to exhibit the character of my automatic pistol, and I had never used it here, but before I started on this journey I decided to give them an example of its power, and possibly awe them. Inviting the Chief and all the tribe to witness my experiment, I explained to them that this little weapon would make a great noise and bore a hole through a thick tree. The Chief examined it gingerly after I had locked the trigger mechanism. He had heard of such arms, he said, but thought that they were much larger and heavier. This one, he thought, must be a baby and he was inclined to doubt its power.

Selecting an "assai" palm of about nine inches diameter, across the creek, I took steady aim and fired four bullets. Three of the bullets went through the same hole and the fourth pierced the trunk of the palm about two inches higher. The Chief and his men hurried across the creek and examined the holes which caused then to discuss the affair for more than an hour. The empty shells which had been ejected from the magazine were picked up by two young girls who fastened them in their ears with wire-like fibres, whereupon a dozen other women surrounded me, beseeching me to give them also cartridge-shells. I discharged more than a dozen bullets, to please these children of the forest, who were as completely the slaves of fashion as are their sisters of more civilised lands.

Early the next morning we started up the river. In one canoe the Chief and I sat on jaguar skins, while two men paddled. In another canoe were four men armed with bows and arrows and blow-guns, and a fifth who acted in the capacity of "Wireless Operator." The system of signalling which he employed was by far the most ingenious device I saw while in Brazil, and considering their resources and their low state of culture the affair was little short of marvellous.

Before the canoes were launched, a man fastened two upright forked sticks on each side of one, near the middle. About three and a half feet astern of these a cross-piece was laid on the bottom of the craft. To this was attached two shorter forked sticks. Between each pair of upright forked sticks was placed another cross-piece, thus forming two horizontal bars, parallel to each other, one only a few inches from the bottom of the boat and the other about a foot and a half above the gunwales. Next, four slabs of Caripari wood of varying thickness, about three feet long and eight inches wide, were suspended from these horizontal bars, so as to hang lengthwise of the canoe and at an angle of forty-five degrees. Each pair of slabs was perforated by a longitudinal slit and they were joined firmly at their extremities by finely carved and richly painted end-pieces.

The operator strikes the slabs with a wooden mallet or hammer, the head of which is wrapped with an inch layer of caoutchouc and then with a cover of thick tapir-skin. Each section of the wooden slabs gives forth a different note when struck, a penetrating, xylophonic, tone but devoid of the disagreeably metallic, disharmonic bysounds of that instrument. The slabs of wood were suspended by means of thin fibre-cords from the crosspieces, and in this manner all absorption by the adjacent material was done away with.

By means of many different combinations of the four notes obtained which, as far as I could ascertain, were *Do--Re--Mi--Fa*, the operator was able to send any message to a person who understood this code. The operator seized one mallet with each hand and gave the thickest section, the *Do* slat, a blow, followed by a blow with the left hand mallet on the *Re* slat; a blow on the *Mi* slat and on the *Fa* slat followed in quick succession. These four notes, given rapidly and repeated several times, represented the tuning up of the "wireless," calculated to catch the attention of the operator at the *maloca* up-creek. The sound was very powerful, but rather pleasant, and made the still forest resound with a musical echo. He repeated this tuning process several times, but received no answer and we proceeded for a mile. Then we stopped and signalled again. Very faintly came a reply from some invisible source. I learned afterwards that at this time we were at least five miles from the answering station. As soon as communication was thus established the first message was sent through the air, and it was a moment of extreme suspense for me when the powerful notes vibrated through the depth of the forest. I shall never forget this message, not only because it was ethnographically interesting, but because so much of my happiness depended upon a favourable reply. I made the operator repeat it for my benefit when we later returned to our village, and I learned it by heart by whistling it. When printed it looks like this:

After each message the operator explained its meaning. The purport of this first message was so important to me that I awaited the translation with much the same feelings that a prisoner listens for the verdict of the jury when it files back into the court-room.

Questions and answers now came in rapid succession. "A white man is coming with us; he seems to have a good heart, and to be of good character."

Whereupon the deciding answer was translated: "You are all welcome provided you place your arms in the bottom of the canoe."

Next message: "We ask you to place your arms in the *maloca*; we are friends."

After the last message we paddled briskly ahead, and at the end of one hour's work we made a turn of the creek and saw a large open space where probably five hundred Indians had assembled outside of two round *malocas*, constructed like ours. How much I now regretted leaving my precious camera out in the forest, but that was a thing of the past and the loss could not be repaired. The view that presented itself to my eyes was a splendid and rare one for a civilised man to see. The crowd standing on the banks had never seen a white man before; how would they greet me?

Little dogs barked, large scarlet *araras* screamed in the tree-tops, and the little children hid themselves behind their equally fearful mothers. The tribal Chief, a big fellow, decorated with squirrel tails and feathers of the *mutum* bird around, his waist and with the tail feathers of the scarlet and blue *arara*-parrot adorning his handsome head, stood in front with his arms folded.

We landed and the operator dismantled his musical apparatus and laid it carefully in the bottom of the canoe. The two Chiefs embraced each other, at the same time uttering their welcome greeting "*He--He*." I was greeted in the same cordial manner and we all entered the Chief's *maloca* in a long procession. Here in the village of the kindred tribe we stayed for two days, enjoying unlimited hospitality and kindness. Most of the time was spent eating, walking around the *malocas*, looking at dugouts, and at the farinha plants.

On the third day we went back to our *maloca* where I prepared for my return trip to civilisation. It was now the beginning of October.

I would, finally, have recorded many words of the Mangeroma language had not my pencil given out after I had been there a month. The pencil was an "ink-pencil," that is, a pencil with a solid "lead" of bluish colour, very soft, sometimes called "indelible pencil." This lead became brittle from the moisture of the air and broke into fragments so that I could do nothing with it, and my recording was at an end. Fortunately I had made memoranda covering the life and customs before this.

CHAPTER X
THE FIGHT BETWEEN THE MANGEROMAS AND THE PERUVIANS

I was sitting outside the *maloca* writing my observations in the note-book which I always carried in my hunting-coat, when two young hunters hurried toward the Chief, who was reclining in the shade of a banana-tree near the other end of the large house. It was early afternoon, when most of the men of the Mangeromas were off hunting in the near-by forests, while the women and children attended to various duties around the village. Probably not more than eight or ten men remained about the *maloca*.

I had recovered from my sickness and was not entirely devoid of a desire for excitement--the best tonic of the explorer. The two young hunters with bows and arrows halted before the Chief. They were gesticulating wildly; and although I could not understand what they were talking about, I judged from the frown of the Chief that something serious was the matter.

He arose with unusual agility for a man of his size, and shouted something toward the opening of the *maloca*, whence the men were soon seen coming with leaps and bounds. Anticipating trouble, I also ran over to the Chief, and, in my defective Mangeroma lingo, inquired the cause of the excitement. He did not answer me, but, in a greater state of agitation than I had previously observed in him, he gave orders to his men. He called the "wireless" operator and commanded him to bring out his precious apparatus. This was soon fastened to the gunwales of the canoe where I had seen it used before, on my trip to the neighbouring tribe, and soon the same powerful, xylophonic sounds vibrated through the forest. It was his intention to summon the hunters that were still roaming around the vicinity, by this "C.Q.D." message. The message I could not interpret nor repeat, although it was not nearly as complex as the one I had learned before. After a while, the men came streaming into the *maloca* from all directions, with anxiety darkening their faces. I had now my first inkling of what was the cause of the commotion, and it did not take me long to understand that we were in danger from some Peruvian *caboclos*. The two young men who had brought the news to the Chief had spied a detachment of Peruvian half-breeds as they were camping in our old *tambo* No. 6, the one we had built on our sixth day out from Floresta. There were about a score of them, all ugly *caboclos*, or half-breed *caucheros*, hunting rubber and no doubt out also for prey in the shape of young Mangeroma girls, as was their custom. The traps set by the Indians, as described in a previous chapter, would be of no avail in this case, as the number of Peruvians was greater than in any previous experience.

The enemy had been observed more than ten miles off, in an easterly direction, when our two hunters were on the trail of a large herd of peccaries, or wild boars, they had sighted in the early morning. The Peruvians were believed to be heading for the *maloca* of the Mangeromas, as there were no other settlements in this region excepting the up-creek tribe, but this numbered at least five hundred souls, and would be no easy prey for them.

I now had a remarkable opportunity to watch the war preparations of these savage, cannibal people, my friends, the Mangeromas. Their army consisted of twelve able-bodied men, all fine muscular fellows, about five feet ten in height, and bearing an array of vicious-looking weapons such as few white men have seen. First of all were three club-men, armed with strong, slender clubs, of hard and extremely tough Caripari wood. The handle, which was very slim, was provided with a knob at the end to prevent the club from slipping out of the hand when in action. The heavy end was furnished with six bicuspid teeth of the black jaguar, embedded in the wood and projecting about two inches beyond the surface. The club had a total length of five feet and weighed about eight pounds. The second division of the wild-looking band consisted of three spear-men, each provided with the three-pronged spears, a horrible weapon which always proves fatal in the hands of these savages. It is a long straight shaft of Caripari wood, about one inch in thickness, divided into three parts at the end, each division being tipped with a barbed bone of the sting-ray. These bones, about three and a half inches long, were smeared with wourahli poison, and thus rendered absolutely fatal even when inflicting only a superficial wound. Each man carried two of these spears, the points being protected by grass-sheaths. The third division was composed of three bow-and-arrow men, the youngest men in the tribe, boys of sixteen and seventeen. They were armed with bows of great length, from six to seven feet, and each bore, at his left side, a quiver, containing a dozen big-game arrows fully five feet long. These arrows, as far as I could ascertain, were not poisoned, but their shock-giving and rending powers were extraordinary. The arrow-heads were all made of the bones of the sting-ray, in themselves formidable weapons, because of the many jagged barbs that prevent extraction from a wound except by the use of great force, resulting in ugly laceration.

The fourth and last division consisted of three blow-gun men, the most effective and cunning of this deadly and imposing array. As so much depended upon the success of a first attack on the Peruvians, who not only outnumbered us, but also were armed with Winchesters, the blow-guns were in the hands of the older and more experienced men. All, except the club-men, wore, around the waist, girdles fringed with *mutum* plumes, and the captains added, to their uniforms multi-coloured fringes of squirrel tails. Their faces all had the usual scarlet and black stripes. The Chief, and his principal aide, or sub-Chief, had on their gayest feathers, including head ornaments of *arara* plumes and egrets. The club-men were naked, except for their head-gear, which consisted simply of a band of *mutum* plumes. When the warriors stood together in their costumes, ready for battle, they presented an awe-inspiring sight.

The Chief gave the order for the bow-and-arrow men to start in single file, the others to follow after, in close succession. The Chief and I fell in at the rear. In the meantime I had examined my Luger automatic pistol to make sure of the smooth action of the mechanism, and found besides that I had in all thirty-seven soft-nose bullets. This was my only weapon, but previous narrow escapes from death and many close contacts with danger had hardened me, so I was willing to depend entirely upon my pistol. The women and children of the *maloca* stood around, as we disappeared in the jungle, and, while they showed some interest in the proceeding, they displayed little or no emotion. A couple of sweethearts exchanged kisses as composedly as if they had been bluecoats parting with the ladies of their choice before going to the annual parade.

Soon we were in the dark, dense jungle that I was now so well acquainted with, and, strange to say, the green and tangled mass of vegetation contained more terrors for me than the bloody combat that was to follow.

For an hour we travelled in a straight line, pushing our way as noiselessly as possible through the thick mass of creepers and lianas. About three o'clock, one of the scouts sighted the Peruvians, and our Chief decided that an attack should be made as soon as possible, before darkness could set in. We stopped and sent out two bow-and-arrow men to reconnoitre. An anxious half hour passed before one of them returned with the report that the Peruvians were now coming towards us and would probably reach our position in a few minutes. I could almost hear my heart thump; my knees grew weak, and for a moment I almost wished that I had stayed in the *maloca*.

The Chief immediately directed certain strategic movements which, in ingenuity and foresight, would have been worthy of a Napoleon.

We were between two low hills, covered with the usual dense vegetation, which made it impossible to see an advancing enemy at a distance of more than five yards. The three blow-gun men were now ordered to ascend the hills on each side of the valley and conceal themselves about half-way up the slopes, and towards the enemy. They were to insert the poisoned arrows in their guns and draw a bead on the Peruvians as they came on cutting their way through the underbrush. The bow-and-arrow men posted themselves farther on about five yards behind the blow-gun men, with big-game arrows fitted to the bowstrings, ready to shoot when the first volley of the deadly and silent poisoned arrows had been fired. Farther back were the spear-men with spears unsheathed, and finally came the three brave and ferocious club-men. Of these last warriors, a tall athlete was visibly nervous, not from fear but from anticipation. The veins of his forehead stood out, pulsating with every throb of his heart. He clutched the heavy club and continually gritted his white, sharp-filed teeth in concentrated rage. It was wisely calculated that the Peruvians would unconsciously wedge themselves into this trap, and by the time they could realise their danger their return would be cut off by our bow-and-arrow men in their rear.

After a pause that seemed an eternity to most of us no doubt, for the savage heart beats as the white man's in time of danger and action, we heard the talking and shouting of the enemy as they advanced, following the natural and easiest route between the hills and cutting their way through the brush. I stood near the Chief and the young club-man Arara, who, on account of his bravery and great ability in handling his club, had been detailed to remain near us.

Before I could see any of the approaching foe, I heard great shouts of anger and pain from them. It was easy for me to understand their cries as they spoke Spanish and their cursings sounded loud through the forest.

The blow-gun men, perceiving the Peruvians at the foot of the hill only some twenty feet away, had prudently waited until at least half a dozen were visible, before they fired a volley of poisoned arrows. The three arrows fired in this first volley all hit their mark. Hardly had they gone forth, when other arrows were dexterously inserted in the tubes. The work of the blow-gun men was soon restricted to the picking out of any stray enemy, their long, delicate, and cumbersome blow-guns preventing them from taking an active part in the melee. Now the conflict was at its height and it was a most remarkable one, on account of its swiftness and fierceness. The bow-and-arrow men charging with their sting-ray arrows poisoned with the wourahli took the place of the cautiously retreating blow-gun men. At the same instant the spear-men rushed down, dashing through the underbrush at the foot of the hill, like breakers on a stormy night.

The rear-guard of the Peruvians now came into action, having had a chance to view the situation. Several of them filed to the right and managed to fire their large-calibre bullets into the backs of our charging bow-and-arrow men, but, in their turn, they were picked off by the blow-gun men, who kept firing their poisoned darts from a safe distance. The fearful yells of our men, mingled with the cursing of the Peruvians, and the sharp reports of their heavy rifles, so plainly heard, proved that the centre of battle was not many yards from the spot where I was standing.

The club-men now broke into action; they could not be kept back any longer. The tension had already been too painful for these brave fellows, and with fierce war-cries of "*Yob--Hee--Hee*" they launched themselves into the fight, swinging their strong clubs above their heads and crashing skulls from left to right. By this time the Peruvians had lost many men, but the slaughter went on. The huge black clubs of the Mangeromas fell again and again, with sickening thuds, piercing the heads and brains of the enemy with the pointed jaguar teeth.

Suddenly two Peruvians came into view not more than twelve feet from where the Chief, Arara the big club-man, and I were standing. One of these was a Spaniard, evidently the captain of this band of marauders (or, to use their correct name, *caucheros*). His face was of a sickly, yellowish hue, and a big, black moustache hid the lower part of his cruel and narrow chin. He took a quick aim as he saw us in his path, but before he could pull the trigger, Arara, with a mighty side-swing of his club literally tore the Spaniard's head off. Now, at last, the bonds of restraint were broken for this handsome devil Arara, and yelling himself hoarse, and with his strong but cruel face contracted to a fiendish grin, he charged the enemy; I saw him crush the life out of three.

The Chief took no active part in the fight whatever, but added to the excitement by bellowing with all his might an encouraging "*Aa--Oo--Ah*." No doubt, this had a highly beneficial effect upon the tribesmen, for they never for an instant ceased their furious fighting until the last Peruvian was killed. During the final moments of the battle, several bullets whirred by me at close range, but during the whole affair I had had neither opportunity nor necessity for using my pistol. Now, however, a *caboclo*, with a large, bloody machete in his hand, sprang from behind a tree and made straight for me. I dodged behind another tree and saw how the branches were swept aside as he rushed towards me.

Then I fired point-blank, sending three bullets into his head. He fell on his face at my feet. As I bent over him, I saw that he had a blow-gun arrow in his left thigh; he was therefore a doomed man before he attacked me. This was my first and only victim, during this brief but horrible slaughter. As I was already thoroughly sick from the noise of cracking rifles and the thumping of clubs smashing their way into the brains of the Peruvians, I rushed toward the centre of the valley where the first attack on the advance guard of the enemy had taken place, but even more revolting was the sight that revealed itself. Here and there bushes were shaking as some *caboclo* crawled along on all fours in his death agony. Those who were struck by the blow-gun arrows seemed simply to fall asleep without much pain or struggle, but the victims of the club-men and the bow-and-arrow men had a terrible death. They could not die by the merciful wourahli poison, like those shot by the blow-gun, but expired from hemorrhages caused by the injuries of the ruder weapons. One poor fellow was groaning most pitifully. He had received a well-directed big-game arrow in the upper part of the abdomen, the arrow having been shot with such terrible force that about a foot of the shaft projected from the man's back. The arrow-head had been broken off by striking a vertebra.

The battle was over. Soon the ***urubus***, or vultures, were hanging over the tree-tops waiting for their share of the spoils. The men assembled in front of the Chief for roll-call. Four of our men were killed outright by rifle-bullets, and it was typical of these brave men that none were killed by machete stabs. The entire marauding expedition of twenty Peruvians was completely wiped out, not a single one escaping the deadly aim of the Mangeromas. Thus was avoided the danger of being attacked in the near future by a greater force of Peruvians, called to this place from the distant frontier by some returning survivor.

It is true that the Mangeromas lay in ambush for their enemy and killed them, for the greater part, with poisoned arrows and spears, but the odds were against the Indians, not only because the ***caboclos*** were attacking them in larger numbers, but because they came with modern, repeating fire-arms against the hand weapons of the Mangeromas. These marauders, too, came with murder and girl-robbery in their black hearts, while the Mangeromas were defending their homes and families. But it is true that after the battle, so bravely fought, the Indians cut off the hands and feet of their enemies, dead or dying, and carried them home.

The fight lasted only some twenty minutes, but it was after sunset when we reached the ***maloca***. The women and children received us with great demonstrations of joy. Soon the pots and pans were boiling inside the great house. I have previously observed how the Mangeromas would partake of parts of the human body as a sort of religious rite, whenever they had been successful with their man-traps; now they feasted upon the hands and feet of the slain, these parts having been distributed among the different families.

I crept into my hammock and lit my pipe, watching the great mass of naked humanity. All the men had laid aside their feather-dresses and squirrel tails, and were moving around among the many fires on the floor of the hut. Some were sitting in groups discussing the battle, while women bent over the pots to examine the ghastly contents. Here, a woman was engaged in stripping the flesh from the palm of a hand and the sole of a foot, which operation finished, she threw both into a large earthen pot to boil; there, another woman was applying an herb-poultice to her husband's wounds.

Over it all hung a thick, odoriferous smoke, gradually finding its way out through the central opening in the roof.

This was a feast, indeed, such as few white men, I believe, have witnessed.

That night and the next day, and the following four days, great quantities of *chicha* were drunk and much meat was consumed to celebrate the great victory, the greatest in the annals of the Mangeromas of Rio Branco.

Earthen vessels and jars were used in the cooking of food. The red clay (Tabatinga clay) found abundantly in these regions formed a superior material for these utensils. They were always decorated symbolically with juices of the scarlet *urucu* and the black *genipapa*. Even when not burned into the clay, these were permanent colours.

Men and women wore their hair long and untrimmed as far as I could observe. The older and more experienced of the tribesmen would have quite elaborate headgear, consisting of a band of *mutum* plumes, interspersed with parrot-tail feathers, while the younger hunters wore nothing but a band of the *mutum* plumes. The body was uncovered, save by a narrow strip of bark encircling the waist. A broad piece, woven of several bark-strips into a sort of mat, protected the lower anterior part of the abdomen. The women wore no clothing whatever.

Their colour was remarkably light. Probably nothing can designate this better than the statement that if a Mangeroma were placed alongside of an Italian, no difference would be noticeable. Their cheek-bones were not as high as is usual with tribes found on the Amazon; they seemed to come from a different race. Their eyes were set straight without any tendency to the Mongolian slanting that characterises the Peruvian *caboclos* and the tribes of the northern affluents. The women had unusually large feet, while those of the men were small and well-shaped. The general appearance of a young Mangeroma was that of a well-proportioned athlete, standing about five feet ten in his bare feet. No moccasins, nor any other protection for the feet, were worn.

The supply of wourahli poison had run low and three wourahli men were to go out in the forest to collect poison plants, a journey which would require several days to complete. This occasion was set as the time of my departure.

It was a rainy morning when I wrapped my few belongings in a leaf, tied some grass-fibres around them, and inserted them in the large pocket of my khaki-coat. The box with the gold dust was there, also the boxes with the exposed photographic plates. Most of the gold had filtered out of the box, but a neat quantity still remained. One of my servants--a handsome girl--who, excepting for the labial ornaments, could have been transformed into an individual of quite a civilised appearance by opportunity, gave me a beautiful black necklace as a souvenir. It was composed of several hundred pieces, all carved out of ebony nuts. It had cost her three weeks of constant work. I embraced and was embraced by almost everybody in the *maloca*, after which ceremony we went in procession to the canoe that was to take me down to the Branco River. The Chief bade me a fond farewell, that forever shall be implanted in my heart. I had lived here weeks among these cannibal Indians, had enjoyed their kindness and generosity without charge; I could give them nothing in return and they asked nothing. I could have stayed here for the rest of my natural life if I had so desired, but now I was to say good-bye forever. How wonderful was this farewell! It was my opportunity for acknowledging that the savage heart is by no means devoid of the feelings and sentiments that characterise more elevated, so-called civilised individuals.

For the last time I heard the little dog bark, the same that had licked my face when I fainted in front of the *maloca* upon my first arrival; and the large *arara* screamed in the tree-tops as I turned once more towards the world of the white man.

The journey was without incident. The wourahli men set me off near the mouth of the Branco River, at a distance which I covered in less than five hours by following the banks. I was greeted by Coronel Maya of the *Compagnie Transatlantique de Caoutchouc*, who sent me by canoe down the old Itecoahy, until we reached the Floresta headquarters.

Here I gave Coronel da Silva an account of the death of Chief Marques, and the brave Jerome, which made a deep impression upon this noble man.

The three men, Magellaes, Anisette, and Freitas, had returned in safety after they separated from us.

I met the wife of Chief Marques. She was the woman whose arm I had amputated. When I saw her she was carrying, with the arm left to her, a pail of water from the little creek behind headquarters. She was a different woman, and I was pleased to know that my desperate surgical operation had resulted so well. Her cheeks were full and almost rosy. Her health, I was told, excepting for occasional attacks of ague, was very good.

Soon after, the launch arrived from Remate de Males and I put my baggage on board. The Coronel accompanied me down river for about forty-eight hours and then, reaching the northern extremity of his estate, he bade me a fond good-bye with the words: "***Sempre, illustrissimo Senhor, minha casa e a suas ordenes***," "My house, most illustrious Sir, is always at your disposal."

When I arrived at Remate de Males I had another attack of malaria, which almost severed the slender thread by which my life hung; my physical resistance was gone. But I managed to develop my plates before breaking down completely, and after having disposed of my small quantity of gold dust, for which I realised some three hundred and forty dollars, I was taken down to the mouth of the Javary River, where I had landed almost a year previous, now a physical and, I might almost say, mental wreck. I stayed in the house of Coronel Monteiro, the frontier official at Esperanca, for five long days, fighting with death, until one afternoon I saw the white hull of the R.M.S. ***Napo*** appear at a bend of the Amazon, only five hundred yards away.

Closer she came--this rescuing instrument of Providence. She was none too soon, for I had now reached the last notch of human endurance. She dropped anchor; a small gasoline launch was lowered into the water; three white-coated officers stepped into it--they came ashore--they climbed the stairs. The captain, a stout, kind-looking Englishman, approached my hammock and found therein a very sick white man. I was carried aboard and placed in the hands of the ship's physician. At last those black forests of the Amazon were left behind. After twenty-two days' sail, Sandy Hook lighthouse loomed on our port side, and soon after, I could rest--rest, and ***live*** again!

The Codes Of Hammurabi And Moses
W. W. Davies

QTY

The discovery of the Hammurabi Code is one of the greatest achievements of archaeology, and is of paramount interest, not only to the student of the Bible, but also to all those interested in ancient history...

Religion   ISBN: *1-59462-338-4*   **Pages:132**
MSRP $12.95

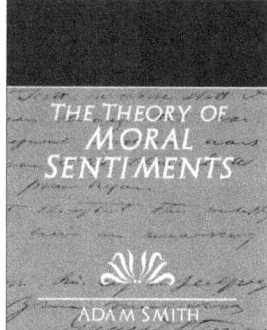

The Theory of Moral Sentiments
Adam Smith

QTY

This work from 1749. contains original theories of conscience amd moral judgment and it is the foundation for systemof morals.

Philosophy ISBN: *1-59462-777-0*   **Pages:536**
MSRP $19.95

Jessica's First Prayer
Hesba Stretton

QTY

In a screened and secluded corner of one of the many railway-bridges which span the streets of London there could be seen a few years ago, from five o'clock every morning until half past eight, a tidily set-out coffee-stall, consisting of a trestle and board, upon which stood two large tin cans, with a small fire of charcoal burning under each so as to keep the coffee boiling during the early hours of the morning when the work-people were thronging into the city on their way to their daily toil...

Pages:84

Childrens   ISBN: *1-59462-373-2*   *MSRP $9.95*

My Life and Work
Henry Ford

QTY

Henry Ford revolutionized the world with his implementation of mass production for the Model T automobile. Gain valuable business insight into his life and work with his own auto-biography... "We have only started on our development of our country we have not as yet, with all our talk of wonderful progress, done more than scratch the surface. The progress has been wonderful enough but..."

Pages:300

Biographies/ ISBN: *1-59462-198-5*   *MSRP $21.95*

The Art of Cross-Examination
Francis Wellman

QTY

I presume it is the experience of every author, after his first book is published upon an important subject, to be almost overwhelmed with a wealth of ideas and illustrations which could readily have been included in his book, and which to his own mind, at least, seem to make a second edition inevitable. Such certainly was the case with me; and when the first edition had reached its sixth impression in five months, I rejoiced to learn that it seemed to my publishers that the book had met with a sufficiently favorable reception to justify a second and considerably enlarged edition. ...

Reference   ISBN: *1-59462-647-2*

Pages:412

MSRP $19.95

On the Duty of Civil Disobedience
Henry David Thoreau

QTY

Thoreau wrote his famous essay, On the Duty of Civil Disobedience, as a protest against an unjust but popular war and the immoral but popular institution of slave-owning. He did more than write—he declined to pay his taxes, and was hauled off to gaol in consequence. Who can say how much this refusal of his hastened the end of the war and of slavery ?

Law   ISBN: *1-59462-747-9*

Pages:48

MSRP $7.45

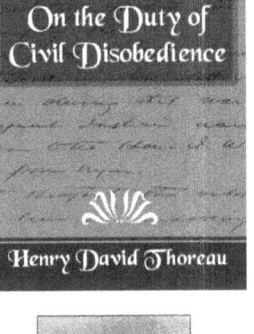

Dream Psychology Psychoanalysis for Beginners
Sigmund Freud

QTY

Sigmund Freud, born Sigismund Schlomo Freud (May 6, 1856 - September 23, 1939), was a Jewish-Austrian neurologist and psychiatrist who co-founded the psychoanalytic school of psychology. Freud is best known for his theories of the unconscious mind, especially involving the mechanism of repression; his redefinition of sexual desire as mobile and directed towards a wide variety of objects; and his therapeutic techniques, especially his understanding of transference in the therapeutic relationship and the presumed value of dreams as sources of insight into unconscious desires.

Dream Psychology
Psychoanalysis for Beginners

Sigmund Freud

Psychology   ISBN: *1-59462-905-6*

Pages:196

MSRP $15.45

The Miracle of Right Thought
Orison Swett Marden

QTY

Believe with all of your heart that you will do what you were made to do. When the mind has once formed the habit of holding cheerful, happy, prosperous pictures, it will not be easy to form the opposite habit. It does not matter how improbable or how far away this realization may see, or how dark the prospects may be, if we visualize them as best we can, as vividly as possible, hold tenaciously to them and vigorously struggle to attain them, they will gradually become actualized, realized in the life. But a desire, a longing without endeavor, a yearning abandoned or held indifferently will vanish without realization.

Pages:360

Self Help   ISBN: *1-59462-644-8*

MSRP $25.45

☐ **The Rosicrucian Cosmo-Conception Mystic Christianity** *by Max Heindel*　ISBN: *1-59462-188-8*　**$38.95**
The Rosicrucian Cosmo-conception is not dogmatic, neither does it appeal to any other authority than the reason of the student. It is: not controversial, but is: sent forth in the, hope that it may help to clear...　　　　　　　　　　　　　　　　　　　　　New Age/Religion Pages 646

☐ **Abandonment To Divine Providence** *by Jean-Pierre de Caussade*　ISBN: *1-59462-228-0*　**$25.95**
"The Rev. Jean Pierre de Caussade was one of the most remarkable spiritual writers of the Society of Jesus in France in the 18th Century. His death took place at Toulouse in 1751. His works have gone through many editions and have been republished...　　　Inspirational/Religion Pages 400

☐ **Mental Chemistry** *by Charles Haanel*　ISBN: *1-59462-192-6*　**$23.95**
Mental Chemistry allows the change of material conditions by combining and appropriately utilizing the power of the mind. Much like applied chemistry creates something new and unique out of careful combinations of chemicals the mastery of mental chemistry...　　　　New Age Pages 354

☐ **The Letters of Robert Browning and Elizabeth Barret Barrett 1845-1846 vol II**　ISBN: *1-59462-193-4*　**$35.95**
by Robert Browning and Elizabeth Barrett　　　　　　　　　　　　　　　　　　　　　　　　　　　Biographies Pages 596

☐ **Gleanings In Genesis (volume I)** *by Arthur W. Pink*　ISBN: *1-59462-130-6*　**$27.45**
Appropriately has Genesis been termed "the seed plot of the Bible" for in it we have, in germ form, almost all of the great doctrines which are afterwards fully developed in the books of Scripture which follow...　　　　　　　　　　　　　　　　Religion/Inspirational Pages 420

☐ **The Master Key** *by L. W. de Laurence*　ISBN: *1-59462-001-6*　**$30.95**
In no branch of human knowledge has there been a more lively increase of the spirit of research during the past few years than in the study of Psychology, Concentration and Mental Discipline. The requests for authentic lessons in Thought Control, Mental Discipline and...　New Age/Business Pages 422

☐ **The Lesser Key Of Solomon Goetia** *by L. W. de Laurence*　ISBN: *1-59462-092-X*　**$9.95**
This translation of the first book of the "Lernegton" which is now for the first time made accessible to students of Talismanic Magic was done, after careful collation and edition, from numerous Ancient Manuscripts in Hebrew, Latin, and French...　　　　　New Age/Occult Pages 92

☐ **Rubaiyat Of Omar Khayyam** *by Edward Fitzgerald*　ISBN: *1-59462-332-5*　**$13.95**
Edward Fitzgerald, whom the world has already learned, in spite of his own efforts to remain within the shadow of anonymity, to look upon as one of the rarest poets of the century, was born at Bredfield, in Suffolk, on the 31st of March, 1809. He was the third son of John Purcell...　Music Pages 172

☐ **Ancient Law** *by Henry Maine*　ISBN: *1-59462-128-4*　**$29.95**
The chief object of the following pages is to indicate some of the earliest ideas of mankind, as they are reflected in Ancient Law, and to point out the relation of those ideas to modern thought.　　　　　　　　　　　　　　　　　　　　Religiom/History Pages 452

☐ **Far-Away Stories** *by William J. Locke*　ISBN: *1-59462-129-2*　**$19.45**
"Good wine needs no bush, but a collection of mixed vintages does. And this book is just such a collection. Some of the stories I do not want to remain buried for ever in the museum files of dead magazine-numbers an author's not unpardonable vanity..."　　　　Fiction Pages 272

☐ **Life of David Crockett** *by David Crockett*　ISBN: *1-59462-250-7*　**$27.45**
"Colonel David Crockett was one of the most remarkable men of the times in which he lived. Born in humble life, but gifted with a strong will, an indomitable courage, and unremitting perseverance...　　　　　　　　　　　　　　Biographies/New Age Pages 424

☐ **Lip-Reading** *by Edward Nitchie*　ISBN: *1-59462-206-X*　**$25.95**
Edward B. Nitchie, founder of the New York School for the Hard of Hearing, now the Nitchie School of Lip-Reading, Inc, wrote "LIP-READING Principles and Practice". The development and perfecting of this meritorious work on lip-reading was an undertaking...　　　How-to Pages 400

☐ **A Handbook of Suggestive Therapeutics, Applied Hypnotism, Psychic Science**　ISBN: *1-59462-214-0*　**$24.95**
by Henry Munro　　　　　　　　　　　　　　　　　　　　　　　　　Health/New Age/Health/Self-help Pages 376

☐ **A Doll's House: and Two Other Plays** *by Henrik Ibsen*　ISBN: *1-59462-112-8*　**$19.95**
Henrik Ibsen created this classic when in revolutionary 1848 Rome. Introducing some striking concepts in playwriting for the realist genre, this play has been studied the world over.　　　　　　　　　　　　　　　　　　　　Fiction/Classics/Plays 308

☐ **The Light of Asia** *by sir Edwin Arnold*　ISBN: *1-59462-204-3*　**$13.95**
In this poetic masterpiece, Edwin Arnold describes the life and teachings of Buddha. The man who was to become known as Buddha to the world was born as Prince Gautama of India but he rejected the worldly riches and abandoned the reigns of power when... Religion/History/Biographies Pages 170

☐ **The Complete Works of Guy de Maupassant** *by Guy de Maupassant*　ISBN: *1-59462-157-8*　**$16.95**
"For days and days, nights and nights, I had dreamed of that first kiss which was to consecrate our engagement, and I knew not on what spot I should put my lips..."　　　　　　　　　　　　　　　　　　　　　　Fiction/Classics Pages 240

☐ **The Art of Cross-Examination** *by Francis L. Wellman*　ISBN: *1-59462-309-0*　**$26.95**
Written by a renowned trial lawyer, Wellman imparts his experience and uses case studies to explain how to use psychology to extract desired information through questioning.　　　　　　　　　　　　　　　　How-to/Science/Reference Pages 408

☐ **Answered or Unanswered?** *by Louisa Vaughan*　ISBN: *1-59462-248-5*　**$10.95**
Miracles of Faith in China　　　　　　　　　　　　　　　　　　　　　　　　　Religion Pages 112

☐ **The Edinburgh Lectures on Mental Science (1909)** *by Thomas*　ISBN: *1-59462-008-3*　**$11.95**
This book contains the substance of a course of lectures recently given by the writer in the Queen Street Hall, Edinburgh. Its purpose is to indicate the Natural Principles governing the relation between Mental Action and Material Conditions...　New Age/Psychology Pages 148

☐ **Ayesha** *by H. Rider Haggard*　ISBN: *1-59462-301-5*　**$24.95**
Verily and indeed it is the unexpected that happens! Probably if there was one person upon the earth from whom the Editor of this, and of a certain previous history, did not expect to hear again...　　　　　　　　　　　　　　Classics Pages 380

☐ **Ayala's Angel** *by Anthony Trollope*　ISBN: *1-59462-352-X*　**$29.95**
The two girls were both pretty, but Lucy who was twenty-one who supposed to be simple and comparatively unattractive, whereas Ayala was credited, as her Bombwhat romantic name might show, with poetic charm and a taste for romance. Ayala when her father died was nineteen... Fiction Pages 484

☐ **The American Commonwealth** *by James Bryce*　ISBN: *1-59462-286-8*　**$34.45**
An interpretation of American democratic political theory. It examines political mechanics and society from the perspective of Scotsman James Bryce　　　　　　　　　　　　　　　　　　　　　　　Politics Pages 572

☐ **Stories of the Pilgrims** *by Margaret P. Pumphrey*　ISBN: *1-59462-116-0*　**$17.95**
This book explores pilgrims religious oppression in England as well as their escape to Holland and eventual crossing to America on the Mayflower, and their early days in New England...　　　　　　　　　　　　　　　　History Pages 268

QTY

The Fasting Cure *by Sinclair Upton*   ISBN: *1-59462-222-1* **$13.95**
In the Cosmopolitan Magazine for May, 1910, and in the Contemporary Review (London) for April, 1910, I published an article dealing with my experiences in fasting. I have written a great many magazine articles, but never one which attracted so much attention... New Age/Self Help/Health Pages 164

Hebrew Astrology *by Sepharial*   ISBN: *1-59462-308-2* **$13.45**
In these days of advanced thinking it is a matter of common observation that we have left many of the old landmarks behind and that we are now pressing forward to greater heights and to a wider horizon than that which represented the mind-content of our progenitors... Astrology Pages 144

Thought Vibration or The Law of Attraction in the Thought World   ISBN: *1-59462-127-6* **$12.95**
by William Walker Atkinson   Psychology/Religion Pages 144

Optimism *by Helen Keller*   ISBN: *1-59462-108-X* **$15.95**
Helen Keller was blind, deaf, and mute since 19 months old, yet famously learned how to overcome these handicaps, communicate with the world, and spread her lectures promoting optimism. An inspiring read for everyone... Biographies Inspirational Pages 84

Sara Crewe *by Frances Burnett*   ISBN: *1-59462-360-0* **$9.45**
In the first place, Miss Minchin lived in London. Her home was a large, dull, tall one, in a large, dull square, where all the houses were alike, and all the sparrows were alike, and where all the door-knockers made the same heavy sound... Childrens/Classic Pages 88

The Autobiography of Benjamin Franklin *by Benjamin Franklin*   ISBN: *1-59462-135-7* **$24.95**
The Autobiography of Benjamin Franklin has probably been more extensively read than any other American historical work, and no other book of its kind has had such ups and downs of fortune. Franklin lived for many years in England, where he was agent... Biographies History Pages 332

Name	
Email	
Telephone	
Address	
City, State ZIP	

☐ **Credit Card**   ☐ **Check / Money Order**

Credit Card Number	
Expiration Date	
Signature	

Please Mail to: Book Jungle
PO Box 2226
Champaign, IL 61825
or Fax to: 630-214-0564

ORDERING INFORMATION

web: *www.bookjungle.com*
email: *sales@bookjungle.com*
fax: *630-214-0564*
mail: *Book Jungle PO Box 2226 Champaign, IL 61825*
or PayPal *to sales@bookjungle.com*

Please contact us for bulk discounts

DIRECT-ORDER TERMS

**20% Discount if You Order
Two or More Books**
Free Domestic Shipping!
Accepted: Master Card, Visa,
Discover, American Express